Ain't Going Back to No Cotton Patch

TERRY R. THOMAS

authorHOUSE®

AuthorHouse™
1663 Liberty Drive
Bloomington, IN 47403
www.authorhouse.com
Phone: 1-800-839-8640

Published by AuthorHouse 6/26/2013

ISBN: 978-1-4817-6385-1 (sc)
ISBN: 978-1-4817-6386-8 (hc)
ISBN: 978-1-4817-6387-5 (e)

Library of Congress Control Number: 2013910709

Cover art by Joshua C. Franks

This book is printed on acid-free paper.

*Because of the dynamic nature of the Internet, any
web addresses or links contained in this book may have
changed since publication and may no longer be valid.*

This book is dedicated to:
My wife Barbara of 52 years,
Our daughters Teresa and Tammie,
Our five grandchildren Joshua, General,
Seth, Samuel, and Adriana Pauline.

In Memory of:
My Parents General C and Pauline Thomas
My Brothers: Ronald Thomas, Paul Thomas,
Jerry Thomas, and Harold Thomas

Foreword
WRITTEN BY ALLEN FRANKLIN

This story is set in mid-twentieth century Alabama, in a very rural, somewhat isolated, at least concerning outside cultural influence, community. People worked hard, physically demanding jobs –largely farming and mining. By necessity people, old and young, lived close to the land for both survival and fun.

Although World War II was just ending, a war three quarters of a century earlier still had a much greater impact on the financial struggles, attitudes, and views of the people both black and white of this region.

Strangely enough, some counties in Alabama were dry (and some still are), creating an ideal market place for moonshiners and of course, some industrious souls saw the opportunity to expand into northern states. This led to the need to "cover" shipping of the whiskey with the commodity of the region –agricultural produce, which becomes the central theme of the story.

This story is true to its time and place and is written in the language common to the period in this very rural region of Alabama; with the coarseness and stark realism which could be told only by one who lived it- which the author did.

The author provides an uncensored window into the people, the personal risks they take to "make-a-buck" and the complex, sometimes contradictory relationship between blacks and whites of the rural south. The reader should find both the language and the story educational and entertaining.

Allen Franklin grew up in this same region of Alabama about the same time frame of this story. Franklin went on to earn an advanced degree in Engineering and retire as President CEO and Chairman for one of the largest Fortune 500 companies in the south.

Introduction

World War II was over in August of 1945 and all the boys were coming home from the war. Some were already home and the rest were on their way. The one's that were not going to come home the families were already finding out. Some were buried at sea and on foreign soil. Aunt Johnnie Turner had five sons, four went to war. They would not take all the sons so they left one at home.

She had twins that were in the Navy, Esco and Osco, one in the army and his name was Eck, one in the Marines and his name was Joe. One of the twins got killed in the battle of the Solomon Islands. In the spring of 1946 one of the boys came home. Aunt Johnnie would always throw a party when one of the boys came home whether it was the soldier or the marine. They would always have cake and banana pudding and fried chicken. For the kids, Aunt Johnnie would always make a dishpan full of popcorn balls. Each time one of her sons would come home she would prepare the same. Once they all got home they had a party in honor of the twin that got killed.

Uncle Steve Eller had a son that was killed in North Africa in 1944. They did not get the news until the war was over on March of 1946. One of the main characters of the story is Sam Johnson and his wife Claire. Their son was killed at Pearl Harbor. He was their only son. They had a big general store in Garden City, Alabama and was one of the leaders in the community. This is giving you a background into the times of Early Spring, Garden City, Alabama 1946.

Table of Contents

CHAPTER ONE
Cotton Chopping Time

Acton Bend, Cotton chopping time in early May. A short black guy about 5'5 plowing one mule and his name was Little Willy and a tall black guy named George was also plowing. James Acton, the boss man son, was also plowing a mule. Seventy-five yards over where the hoe hands were chopping cotton. Late in the evening little Willy made it to the end of the row first and decided to yell quitting time. Well the boss man's son James got mad and told little Willy that "you know that daddy tole yall that when he ain't here that I am the boss out here." He looks over to make sure the hoe hands are still working and puts his hands up to his mouth and hollers "Quitting Time!" "Quitting Time!"

A day or two later, on a typical summer day, when several of the farmers were in town sitting out front of the drugstore telling tales to each other, five or six sitting and standing talking about the weather or fishing, when here comes Deacon Brown from the only Baptist church in town. They greet each other and he says "Preacher Adams wants me to talk to you guys about making up money to buy light fixtures for the church. You know we are about to get electricity and Preacher Adams wants the best." Several of the men say "yea we'll help out" and gives him several dollars. After all, the pastor wanted the best. They all wound up giving him something. About that time a man by the name of Joe Steel about 35 years old came running around the corner yelling "Boys, Boys theys a load of Japs at the filling station on the main highway" and Deacon Brown hollered "<u>Son of a Bitch!</u>" They all took off over there. About the time they got over to the station there was a crowd gathered up around the car with about four or five japs in it. Everybody's anger was built up from the war ever since Pearl Harbor. The police was there and had everything kindly under control. They said "alright guys ya'll back off and go on about your business. These is good Japs. Their just traveling through from Philadelphia on their way to California." One old guy hollered "they ain't no good Japs." Old Dan Ledbetter pretty well the town drunk. He made his living doing odd jobs for people, like working in yards and stuff. He came running up with a hoe in his hand hollering "I'm gonna get me a Jap, I'm gonna get me a Jap." The law grabbed him and pulled him back and said "them's good Japs." Old Dan said "ain't no such a thang as a good Jap." "I tried to join to Navy in 1934," Dan was bout 45 years old, "and they wouldn't take me because I was flat feeted, well flat feeted I'm a gonna get me a dad dam Jap." And the police pulled him off to one side. Another guy hollered out, "yall better not stop in Mississippi."

Garden City

Garden City Alabama is in the southern part of Cullman County. And right at the end of the southside is the Mulberry River. Across the river you got Blount County. To the West of Cullman Co is Walker Co and just to the south joining Blount and Walker Co is Jefferson Co where the big city of Birmingham is. All these other counties are dry, but Jefferson Co is wet. Over on the 78 hwy out of Birmingham toward Memphis right inside the Jefferson County Line was 6 or 8 girly dance halls and clubs. It was legal for them to sale beer but it was illegal to sale whiskey. Anytime you got people wanting to drank they gonna want whiskey. And they will get whiskey. There was this guy named Hollis, Bill Hollis. He owned the biggest juke joint on the strip. He had some little one pot moonshiners making whiskey to sale at his location and to sale at the other joints on the strip. Most of the moon shining was in the edge of Jefferson. Any kind of moonshine was illegal. The law got so bad about busting up their stills and in late 45 or early 46 he decided to move out of that area over into Blount co across the Mulberry River. He had some contacts from Garden City so they decided what all they were going to have to do to run the still. His contact that lived right outside Garden City suggested they get niggers to run the still. That way they would do most of the work at night and if the law tried to catch em they wouldn't be able to see them running through the woods at night. They hired Big George as the lead black man. After he was told he could make three or four times the money making whiskey then he decided he would do it. So he hires little Willy and a crew of five or six other niggers to work in the woods. The railroad runs right through Garden City. Mr Sam Johnson's store was on the street along with Prices and McAnnally's. The stores were on the west side of the street and the railroad was on the East side. Prices and McAnnally's stores ran a rolling store. They went out in the country and stop at people's houses selling flour, coffee, dishpans; some folks had no money but, they could sell eggs, chickens and butter and buy what they needed with the money. It didn't make any difference.

Prices and McAnnally's usually get their rolling stores back in the evening and take inventory and reload for the next morning. Prices and McAnnally's were competitors in the grocery store business. You could also buy mule gear, plow lines, and trace chains. They were competitors but they were also good neighbors. They would not run each other's route. They ran their routes five days a week.

Mr Sam Johnson was up the street from the others. He didn't run a rolling store, he was a wholesaler. Things like sugar, fertilizer, seed, and other things. Mr. Sam and Ms. Clara had a black family that lived next to them. The woman named Ruthie would help Ms. Clara around the house and when she was needed and she would help Mr. Sam in the store. Her husband was named Ben Rivers. He worked in the store selling fertilizer. He would also take Mr. Sam's little flat bed truck and deliver fertilize to the farmers who didn't have another way to come get it except on a mule and wagon. Ben and Ruthie had a boy in 1941 and named him Ben and became known as Little Ben. Mr. Sam and Ms.

Clara took after him like he was there own. They had lost their son in the war. They treated him like their own son. When Little Ben got big enough every time you saw Mr. Sam you would see Little Ben. They would go fishing and things like that.

Chapter Three
Whiskey Makin

Getting back to the whiskey making deal, the contact that Hollis had in the community was a little bitty short guy about 5'1" stout as a mule about 40 years old. His name was William black but was known all over the country as Cracker Black. So Hollis could stay at his joint on the strip he was busy getting the set-up in the woods and organizing the niggers. Cracker Black had been in this kind of business most of his life.

They decided to put the still a couple of miles south of the Mulberry River across from the railroad tracks. They could haul their supplies in and the whiskey out with one of the hand pump railroad cars. He could get one from the section foreman out of Bangor. He had good friends there that could arrange it. He planned it that way where there would not be any tracks going into the woods off the main roads so they couldn't find their still.

The time they got a shipment of whiskey ready the plan was to haul it back up the railroad tracks across the mulberry river. There was a big scope of woods between the river and town and they would hide the whiskey in the woods until they got ready to ship it. Hollis was the ramrod of the whole thing. He was the one putting all the money into it. But now Cracker Black was running the show telling all the black folks what they needed to do. He would tell Big George what to do and he would make sure it was done. Cracker made a deal with Mr. Sam Johnson to buy the sugar. Mr. Sam knew that Cracker had been in the business before so he decided not to ask. So he didn't know but, he did know. As far as he knew he was selling sugar.

They finally got all their equipment in the woods and everything they needed to fire up. They decided to start off with a five hundred gallon vat. That was going to be plenty for what they were going to be selling. Cracker got his railroad buggy so they would haul out a little whiskey and carry in a load of sugar or corn, whatever they needed to make the whiskey. All this had to be done at night. Cracker had a deal with the section foremen at Bangor; everybody knew what time the train ran that's usually how they set their clocks. If there was ever a change in the time the train was running he would let Cracker know so the guys wouldn't be on the tracks that night or if it was a North Bound train they could use the south bound tracks.

CHAPTER FOUR

Making a Run

They were really making more whiskey than Hollis needed on the strip. Cracker had some contacts in Memphis. And he told Hollis if he would keep funding the deal and Cracker would keep making the deals that he would start running a car once a week to Memphis. He had a guy up there that ran a lot of shot houses and he knew he could sell the extra whiskey. He would give Hollis his cut. In the meantime Cracker was getting ready to send his car to Memphis. He hired a guy about 23 years old named Red Turner and had just come out of the war. He had bought him a little 41 coup ford that was a pretty good hotrod. The guy was farming with his daddy but, was interested in making extra money with Cracker. They put extra blocks under the springs so when they loaded it down it would not appear low to the ground. Cracker got all that started and shipped out a couple of loads. A business man out of St Louis who was coming to Birmingham a couple times a month got to stopping in over at Hollis' joint on 78 hwy on his way back home Just getting a little taste of night life and whiskey and so forth. He got to asking about that good shine. He didn't ask where it comes from but, Hollis said that it can be got. So the man bought him a gallon or two on the third trip by to carry home with him. He shared it with some of his friends and they claimed that was the best shine he had ever drank in his life. One guy in the crowd was a guy that furnished about 150 shot houses with bonded and bootleg whiskey. He wanted to get some of this good shine. The business man told him he would ask around and see what he could find out. So on his next trip out of Birmingham he stopped in at Hollis' joint. He had a drank or two. He started talking to Bill about his friends and about the guy who furnished the shot houses that he was interested in buying some if he could get enough that would do him any good. Hollis asked "about how much are you talking about?" He said "if he buys he would like to get about at least 300 gallons at a time." Hollis said "I don't know man it would take a big truck, but let me do some checking and see. It would probably be a month before we could be ready to handle the deal." Hollis got in touch with Cracker and told him what the deal was. All the time they have been splitting the difference down the middle except what Hollis bought to sell at his joint. Cracker told him said "yea I can swing it but, it will take about a month to get ready to run that much." Old Cracker was slick and a fast thinker he told Hollis "we will be able to handle it but, it will take a month. Tell them what we have to have a gallon in Alabama, to get it up there. They will have to pay the freight. The watermelons and peaches and cantaloupes will be ready next month this is June. I know a guy who's got a 41 ford tractor with a 28ft foot trailer with sideboards. He hauls all kinds of produce and in the winter he hauls apples out of North Carolina and Virginia into Birmingham. I'm pretty sure I can get him to haul it."

CHAPTER FIVE
Making a Plan

Cracker said to tell the guy up there to make a deal with a produce man up there to take the produce. "We can't just load 300 gallon of whiskey and haul it up the road. We will have to make this look good. We will have all the produce we need right here in the community." Cracker had to get on the ball to get the whiskey made, keep his car running to Memphis each week and get all the materials ready and get them hauled to the location of the still and get ready for the bigger operation.

One day Cracker went over to see Shorty Thomas about the truck and trailer he owned. He lived between Hayden and Bangor in Blount County. He was the one who would haul the produce up. Cracker went by there and asked for Shorty. Mrs. Thomas knew Cracker and told him Shorty was on a trip and when he comes in she would have him come see him. Cracker said "Yea just tell him to come over and see me and if I'm not home I'll be around town somewhere."

Mr. General Thomas had come into town he was a peach grower up on Oak Grove Mountain. He grew peaches and plums. He had come into Mr. Sam's to pick-up fertilizer for the farm. He had brought several of his toe headed boys in with him; He and Ms Pauline had ten boys that ranged in age from about 2 years till about 17-18 years. Mr. Sam spoke "Hey Mr. General I ain't seen you lately, how's the peaches looking?" Mr. General said "It looks like it's going to be a heavy crop it's looking real good. We are just beginning to pick a few. Not sure how the market is going to be but we are selling them. "General and Shorty by the way are brothers. Mr. General had several big trucks that he operated year round to haul apples out of the Carolinas, Virginia, and West Virginia. He operated year round. Mr. Sam says, "How are all them boys doing and Ms. Pauline?" Mr. General said "Well there doing fine, I've got all the boys working picking peaches and working there at the farm."

CHAPTER SIX
Revenuers

In the meantime Cracker had his deal there with Hollis and his car running into Memphis once a week. And it had been going on about a month, month and a half. The revenuers or FBI have people monitoring the action in the shot houses around town. And this happened to be in Memphis to find out how much whiskey comes in and to see where it comes from also to see if much wildcat comes in and a nose around to try to find out where it comes from. This one particular agent was talking to a few folks coming out of the shot houses. He walks up to this black guy that just came out and was higher than a Georgia Pine and he said to him "Is that good whiskey?" and the response was "Yes Suh that's good whiskey." The agent said "Well I guess I'll go in and get me some whiskey." The other fellow said "Yes Suh! Good Alabama Whiskey." Agent said "Alabama?" He said "Yes suh somewheres north of Birmingham." The agent goes on in and has a shot himself, and hoping he could talk to some more of the people to get more information. He leaves there and goes to three more shot houses. Each time he would ask for the wildcat whiskey. He didn't want any of that bonded whiskey. He had to drink some or the folks would get suspicious of him. He visited three or four more that afternoon but didn't really get any more information except that it had come from Alabama. He reports to the FBI in Memphis and let the FBI in Birmingham know that they had whiskey coming from Birmingham into Memphis. The FBI told them what area it might be coming from. This wasn't the first time the revenuers had been in town. They had a good idea what was going on. They sent agents into Walker, Blount, and Cullman and into north Jefferson County. And they would get some kind of old car would buy a car in that county they were working. Each one would have some kind of scheme to keep people from being so suspicious. He did have a Blount county tag and when people would ask he would make out like he was dealing in real estate telling the people he was looking for land for some people in Miami that had money to buy some cheap land for sale. Land wasn't very high back then anyhow.

He started nosing around north Blount County and all around, Garden City, Bangor, Hayden, and Blount Springs trying to see what all he could find out. It was real slow gathering any information. Time went on and some people began to tell things. He would ask questions and began to get answers. He started parking and walking the woods around. Big George and Cracker both had been seeing that car around. It through up a red flag so they got more on there toes with the operation.

He got to hanging out around Prices and McAnnally's store shooting the breeze. One morning he was out at Mr. Sam's store and a load of sugar came in. Probably 150 100 pound bags and several bundles of 5lbs and 10lbs bags. The agent said, "Mr. Sam you sell a lot of sugar don't ye?" Mr. Sam said "yes I sell a lot of sugar." The agent said "yea that sure is a lot of sugar." By this time Mr. Sam was beginning to get suspicious of the guy. Mr. Sam said, "I was talking to Mr. General Thomas the other day and the peach crop and blackberry crop are looking real good this year. And there will be lots of canning going on in July and August. I don't just sell sugar here in my store I furnish sugar for Mr. Henry and Homer Standridge in Hayden, Mr. Ratliff in

Blountsville, and Berkshire in Hanceville. I wholesale to them so my business isn't just retail here local."

Mr. Sam said "this sugar won't last but about a week so I will be getting in another shipment next week. These folks around here can a lot of fruit. Here in Garden City, Cullman, Hayden, Blount Springs, yea these folks sure can a lot of fruit. We sell a world a lot of sugar. "Whether the agent believed it or not it sounded good so he couldn't argue with it. So he couldn't keep on asking questions because he knew he would tip his hand. He eased around town asking about land and check with old people who had land who might need the money. You could buy land for 50, 75, and 100 an acre in that area.

In his talking around to people, some begin to tip him on Big George might know something about what was going on. He had begun to have a lot of money to spend that wasn't normal for him. He wasn't working in the fields anymore. The agent caught big George and Little Willie in town and began to ask them what they were up to. They said they had been doing odd jobs in town and around and that's why you didn't see them much. He told them enough that they knew who he was. He said he worked for the government and if he caught them lying he would send them to Kilby prison or at least back to the cotton patch. Big George looked at him real strong and said, "Suh I ain't going back to no cotton patch."

Big George and Little Willie went on about their business and the agent got in his car and left. Little Willie and Big George got around the corner and lil Willie started dancing and popping himself on the butt singing" I ain't going back to no cotton patch, I ain't going back to no cotton patch, I ain't seen no cotton patch, what cotton patch."

Big George reported what happened to Cracker and Cracker told him said "well I've had my eye on him. He is the one been driving that car we've seen parked on back roads. We got a good deal going on here and it will be hard for one man to find it out.

What we need to do is we got a couple of places where somebody would come in at if they were looking for the still. We need to put one man on the high bluff across the hollow from the still. Then he can cover both places where somebody might be able to come in." He had a piece of broke mirror that they would use to reflect the sun if someone was coming in. When he saw anything that didn't look right he would take that mirror and reflect down and then would give them time to run and hide and get lost in the woods.

CHAPTER SEVEN

Old Dan

Getting back to things was going around town there in Garden City, if you was walking up and down the street if folks were caught up on their crops people would be in town especially on Saturday. Farmers sitting around talking and shooting the bull and you would hear talking about the niggers. Now there wasn't many blacks that lived out in the country. Most of them was from a little town called Colony. Now some of them did live on the farms or close by their boss man, like Big Ben who worked for Mr. Sam. Anyway, you might hear them talk about the niggers and some would talk about the bad niggers. Some would say things like well they ain't all bad niggers, and one guy would say yea, if you got some that like you then you really got something. And late that afternoon old Dan Ledbetter had found where they were hiding the whiskey and he had not told anybody cause he was getting himself a little shine to drink. He was hiding his in his little shack he lived in at the edge of town. He wouldn't get too high cause he knew if they caught him they'd put him in jail. He had an old nigger called Jud and they worked together everyday doing odd jobs. Whatever anybody needed them to do, work in the garden, rake leaves in the fall or cutting bushes back.

Now old Dan and old Judd got in an alley below Dan's house

and started drinking and getting pretty well drunk and the police, they kept two policemen on duty, and they came down there and caught them. They started questioning Dan wanting to know where he had got that whiskey. He told them somebody came through and he bought it from em. They said "don't tell us no lie." He said, "I ain't lying. A man came through and I bought it from him." The police said, "well we gonna carry you and Judd to jail." Said "ya'll drunk. This is a dry town and a dry county so we gonna carry ya'll to jail." Dan said, "Man we ain't drunk," they said, "you are too drunk." And Dan came back with "Well you ain't gonna lock me up with no nigger." And one of the policeman said, "Dan what difference does it make your sittin here dranking out of the same jug." Old Dan said, "Well I always been sociable."

They put them both in the back of the police car and carried them over to the jailhouse and locked them up in the same cell. Old Dan and Judd been there awhile and he leaned over and said "Judd you ain't gonna tell no body we got locked up together are you." And Judd said "Naw Suh I ain't telling nobody," and Dan said "Man I hope you ain't telling nobody I got my reputation you know." Judd was thinking "and yeah I got mine too."

CHAPTER EIGHT

Expanding the Deal

On Saturday night Shorty Thomas came in and had gone to South Georgia loading a load of cantaloupes for Birmingham. He got loaded so he came on in on Saturday night. Mrs. Thomas had told him that Cracker Black had come by and wants you come talk to him. He said "well I'm tired and I think I'll rest tonight and tomorrow and go over and see him on Monday morning." Early Monday morning Shorty got ready and headed over to see Cracker. Went to his house and ah he wasn't there right then, Mrs. Black said "well Shorty he said he'd back in a little bit sit down there on the porch and wait on him." Cracker got back shortly and said "Come on Shorty walk down to the barn with me I want to talk to you a minute." So they walked on to the barn and Cracker told him the plan. They were going to make a load of whiskey to haul to Saint Louis. He knew Shorty had hauled produce to St Louis for years and asked him if he be interested in hauling it. Shorty said "well, I don't know regular freight up there is about 300.00" and Cracker said "well I've done talked to the man who is the ramrod of the whole deal and said he's be willing to pay 550.00."

Before Shorty could say anything else Cracker continued telling him how they planned to load the truck. He had a produce man from St Louis that would come down and buy the produce. Shorty said "Well I know most of the produce men from up there, who is it?" Cracker said, "A Jew by the name of Martin Levine." Shorty said "Yeah I know old Marty. I been knowing him for some years." Cracker said "yeah well that's who is going to be buying the produce. All you'll have to do is pull in and leave the truck sitting where they will load the whiskey. We will have the peaches, watermelons, and cantaloupes to load. All you'll have to do is bring your truck and take my pick-up and go home. When you come back that night the truck will be loaded and all you have to do is take-off. When you get up there they have a big shed there" and Shorty said "yeah I know where that shed is, that's the one on the market?" Cracker said "yeah that's right." Shorty said "yeah you can drive a truck right into the shed there." Cracker said, "Yeah all you have to do is drive the truck into the shed and they will have a pick-up there with a key in it and go to the hotel. They'll let you know when to be back. You can rest up and be ready to go."

Shorty said "Well, that sounds all good" but said, "Man if they caught me they liable to take my truck. That's the only way I got to make a living. I got a little land and mule but, you can't make a living farming corn and cotton with forty acres and a mule." Cracker said "well I'd already thought about that and" said "well Shorty you know him anyhow, whether you do the job or not I know your not going to say anything so I'll go ahead and tell you the plan. You know Bill Hollis over on 78?" Shorty said "well, yeah I know him been knowing him several years." Cracker said "well he is the one putting up the money and knew it would be a stumbling block about your truck so he said that on paper he would buy your truck so what do you think your truck is worth?" Shorty said "well it's worth $2500 hundred dollars trailer and all." Cracker responded, "He said he would be willing to buy your truck and sign a note and pay you 500 hundred dollars down so you would have plenty of money for your trips." Shorty said "well, I got plenty of money for the trips but, I will want that 500 hundred dollars and him to sign a note." Shorty told Cracker that he wanted to think it over a day or two. "He said who do you think you're going to get your produce from?" Cracker said "I've already talked to General Thomas about getting peaches from him. I told him the produce man was coming down to pay him. I also talked to Dan Washburn about the watermelons and told me all they had to do was bring them over and unload them and that Marty would be here to pay them cash. And the next trip he would send the money back by you." Shorty said "what about the cantaloupes?" Cracker said "I haven't talked to anybody yet," Shorty said "well I got a brother-in-law that lives on Oak Grove Mountain Coy Swann and he grows the best cantaloupes up there. People come from out of the Carolinas to buy his cantaloupes." Cracker said, "well talk to him about the cantaloupe deal and we'll see if we can get everything lined up."

Cracker told Shorty that no one was going to know what was going on. General, Dan and Coy don't need to know. All they need to know is their going to bring their peaches, watermelons, and cantaloupes over here and unload on the dock. He said,"We will have a crew that Marty will pay to load the truck. All they got to do is bring their produce over here unload and go home. Everybody don't need to know the plan." Shorty said "no that's right everybody don't need to know."

Cracker said "I already got a lot of the whiskey made and hid in the woods. We gonna try while the produce is in to run a load a week." Shorty said "well I told you I needed a few days to think about it but, let's go ahead and try it and see what happens. I'll get papers drawn up and go on over to Hollis you sure he's gonna do it?" Cracker said "yeah he's gonna do it." Shorty said "well then I will go on over get the down payment so we will have everything right ready to go." Cracker said to go ahead and talk to Coy about the cantaloupes. They had checked the market and seen what everything is bringing. A dollar and a quarter a bushel, three dollars a bushel for peaches, Mr. General said "that would be fine. That's about as much or more then they would get in Birmingham and not have to haul them there." For big watermelons there going to pay forty cents. Shorty said "yea Cracker I'll handle it with the cantaloupes yea 1.25 a bushel is about what there bringing in Birmingham and that's what I got for mine. I believe Coy will be happy with that"

CHAPTER NINE

The Hummingbird

Up through 1945 up to 1946 about all the trains was coal burning steam engines. That steam engine was making all kinds of noise up and down the railroad track and blowing all kinds of smoke. Bout the time the war was over they begin to come out with diesel engines. Most people did not understand what diesels were just that they didn't make as much noise and smoke. The L & N Rail Road started running a diesel passenger train called the "Hummingbird" that would run 80 or 90 miles an hour. It was very pretty and something else to look at. They were running pretty regular about 1946 and a so getting back to the railroad deal where the railroad section man was suppose to let Cracker and Big George know where they would be running that night just all of a sudden the L&N Rail Road decides to run a special out with the Hummingbird out of Nashville to Mobile for the Mardi Gras. They had a lot of people wanting to go so they decided to run. It was late at night when the section man got the word and didn't have time to let Cracker know. He left out to go to Cracker's place to let him know but, by that time Big George and Little Willie had loaded up the pump car with whiskey and was using the south bound tracks because they knew there was a north bound train due at eleven that night. They were using the south bound track. They had been up to unload and had headed back to the woods. They would take the car off the track when they weren't using it. It would take 4 or 5 niggers to pull it off the track. By this time Big George and Little Willy had already loaded up another load of sugar and had headed back down the track and feeling real good. Little Willie was singing "I ain't going back to no cotton patch, I ain't seed no cotton patch." About that time they saw the lights flashing from north. They were real puzzled because there wasn't supposed to be no train. They kept seeing the lights get closer and closer. And Little Willie's eyes got as big as saucers and started to say Big George that's a a a a hu hum hum huming dam bird. They dove off and the Hummingbird hit there buggy going about 80 or 90 mph and tore it all to pieces. The section foreman had gone up there to let Cracker know but there wasn't enough time to get up there and let them know. Their buggy got tore up so they had to pick up all the junk and hid it all in the woods. The next morning Cracker found out what happened so he made another deal with the section foreman to get another buggy.

Big Walt Thomas from Warrior, Alabama was at the throttle on the Hummingbird that night. Another guy by the name of Dave Hanson was his co-engineer and was in the back part of the engine he heard the noise and felt the jolt when they hit that buggy and hollered and said "Big Walt what happened.?" Big Walt said "I don't know for sure but it looked like a couple of niggers had stole them one of them pump cars and was trying to get away with it."

CHAPTER TEN
Peaches in the Crate

About three days after the train wreck had passed. Shorty come by and let Cracker know that he had done got all the paper work done on the truck and got his down payment. Cracker said "I got enough whiskey in the woods to do my run up to Memphis and got enough to make one trip to St Louis." They decided to let Shorty go ahead and coordinate with the farmers about when they would need to get the produce gathered and bring over to the dock at Garden City. And so Cracker said "Well Marty wants that produce in by Thursday night where they can have it unloaded and on display for the Friday morning market. They don't have any refrigeration so they will need to sell it Friday and Saturday so they don't lose any of it." "So Shorty you go and talk to General, Coy and Dan. We have already talked about how many bushels will need so tell them to have everything on the dock by Wednesday afternoon." So Shorty went and talked to the farmers and they all agreed to have it over there.

Cracker sent Marty a telegram to be down there with the money so everything will be lined up. So on Wednesday morning Dan got his crew in the field gathering the melons. Had Len and Jimmy Washburn, Patrick Adams and a couple of his daughters gathering the watermelons. Coy had his four daughters and three

Dutton boys gathering the cantaloupes. General had his boys and extra hands picking the peaches and getting them ready to go. About two o'clock in the afternoon General had his peaches in the crates and loaded on the truck ready to head down the mountain on crooked dirt roads to where there was a paved road that led into Garden City. All the boys started into asking "Daddy can I go Daddy can I go?" He said "Well a couple of you get in here with me in the big truck," a forty-six ford red with black fenders a pretty thing. "Harold," the oldest, "get the rest in the pick-up and they can all help unload." James and Paul were with Mr. General in the big truck. Harold was driving the pick up and Jerry the second oldest was in with Harold with the little boys was in the truck. GC, the twins, Johnny Bert, Larry Joe and Ronald was all in the back. The young boys were happy and tickled to death when they got to ride on a highway, back then that was really something. One of the twins wanted everybody to get some rocks to throw at dogs and mail boxes and such. Harold was following the big truck and got over on 31 highway and busted a sign or two. The twins would holler I got it and the other one would say no I got it. They got over about a half a mile before you cross the Mulberry River Bridge and throwed at a curve sign and Whamm. They didn't see the Garden City Police was backed up in the bushes. He took off after them with sirens screaming. Harold pulled over and ask the officer what was wrong he knew he wasn't speeding, the officer said "No you wasn't but, them boys was throwing rocks at signs." Harold said "Well I'll take care of them I'll whoop them just like their daddy does." The officer said "Well somebody's going to jail." Harold said "Well there they are just load them up and carry them on to jail." The officer said "Well no I want this time but, somebody will if this keeps going on." The twins both said looking at each other "I didn't do it". So any how the police let them go and got to a pretty good straight away and the police shot the juice to it and then that old forty one ford come around them real fast.

He was showing them just what that old car would do. When he had passed and they got to the Mulberry River sign Wham Bam Wham they throwed the rest of their rocks.

They got on up there to the dock behind Mr. Sam Johnson's store. Part of it was next to the woods where they had their whiskey hid out. I think before I mentioned Mr. General had ten boys, so when they got everything unloaded he gave each one of the boys a dime a piece to go into the store and get a drank and a cake or a bar of candy, whatever they wanted. One old guy in the store said "Say there's ten of yall" the boys replied "yes sir." Sam said "There are ten of yall and no girls" and one of the twins hollered out "Momma's a girl."

CHAPTER ELEVEN
The Watchman

All the farmers had got in with there hired help had gotten all the peaches watermelons and cantaloupes unloaded. Marty was there and got them paid and told them if everything went good they'd probably want to do this again next Wednesday. Then he asked them would it be alright if he sent them there money back by Shorty next time. That would save him a trip. They all said that would be fine. He had already talked to Shorty but, he wanted to check with them. All the farmers got their money and loaded up all their folks and headed for home about 4:00. About 4:30 Shorty came in with the big rig and backed it into the dock. Marty was there and Shorty talked to him a little bit and told him when he was going to try to have it in St Louis. Cracker had left his pick-up for Shorty to drive back home. So he left out. About dark or little bit after dark Big George came in with his crew he had him and little Willie and about five more black guys to load the produce and the whiskey.

Cracker showed back up. Now Cracker had an old guy that lived upstairs a few hundred yards from the dock. The old man had one window that faced 31 highway that faced the police station and then the other window that faced the dock. Cracker had it lined up with him to watch for the police while they were

27

loading. He had an old lantern that he would wave in front of the window when he saw the police turn down that street. Cracker had another guy that all he did was watch for the signal. Any time the old man waved the lantern they would just stop with what they were doing and work on produce. Because it was new the law eased around that first night several times. But they didn't cause any trouble. About ten o'clock they had everything loaded. Whiskey was on the bottom and they had some little o slats in the bed where they could put planks over the whiskey and water melons and cantaloupes would be on top of that so there wouldn't be any weight on the whiskey jugs. And they got everything loaded and left. Shorty got over there and took off over toward 78 highway and up through Jasper headed toward Memphis. About 2:30 AM Shorty got to the Mississippi scales right out from Tupelo and they were opened so he pulled in and put his front wheels on the scales and they said he was alright so he pulled his pull wheels on the scales and they told him he was alright. He pulled on up with his trailer wheels. The scale men knew Shorty so they said "Shorty you're a little overloaded on the axle back there." They had already asked him what he had on. So Shorty asked them how much was he over. They replied "Ah about a box of peaches and a couple of watermelons." Shorty said "Oh well I think we can handle that." One of the scale men started to get the produce off. Shorty said "Oh no let me get up there and get it. I know how it's loaded and if you pull some them from inside the stack said that thing is liable to slide and bust a bunch of watermelons." So they said ok. They had been knowing Shorty a long time and were sort of like buddies so Shorty wasn't afraid of getting in any trouble with them. They were standing around talking a few minutes and wanted to know where he was going with the load and he said Shorty said St Louis. Another guy was walking around the truck and yelled out "Shorty you got something leaking over here." Shorty started around there when the guy reached down and got some of it on his finger and smelled of it and said "Dad Gum it sure smells like whiskey." Shorty went and stuck his finger in it and said "Nah what they've done is put a couple of dead ripe watermelons and them things have soured and blowed out." "When they do them things smell just like whiskey." The old man said "Yea your right they will smell just like whiskey."

CHAPTER TWELVE

Shorty Goes to St Louis

Shorty got out from them and headed on up toward Memphis and across the river at Blival, Arkansas and headed on to St Louis. About 10 o'clock the next morning he was going through this little town Cape Girardo, Missouri right on the bank of the Mississippi river. He was easing through town and had to stop for a red light on a little hill and when he took off the truck was jumping a little because it was a hard pull. The police was watching him and followed him till there was a place to pull off then he put the light on him and hit the siren a couple of times. Shorty pulled over and got out went back to where the cop was at and asked what the trouble was. He said he hadn't run a red light and he sure wasn't speeding. The cop said "Nah I just saw you was loaded a little heavy and thought I might ought to check your truck out." Shorty said "Well that will be fine." The cop was checking the tires and everything. There was still a little bit of whiskey still dripping out so he reached down and smelled of it. He said "Mr. Thomas" he had already checked his license, "that smells like whiskey." "We are going to have to check this out." Shorty said, "Nah I'm loaded with watermelons and cantaloupes and I know what they did they loaded some dead ripe watermelons and they have soured and blowed up and when they leak it smells just like whiskey." The cop said "You might be right but I am going to have to check on it." "We are going to have to unload some of it and see." Shorty said "well I'm not going to unload nothing." The cop said "well we will get somebody to unload it." Shorty didn't figure he had anything to lose so he said "well before you unload anything you bring your mayor around here and sign me a paper that any produce that is damaged this town will have to pay for it." If this makes me late for my appointment and I lose this load that the town will have to pay for that." The cop said "well he ain't going to do that" and Shorty said "well you ain't going to unload no produce." The cop said "Mr. Thomas where you going with this load?" Shorty said "I am going to A&P warehouse in Kansas City." He said "When will you be there?" He said "I will be there on Friday night and their usually there around 6 o'clock Saturday morning to start unloading it." The cop said "I am going to get in touch with the revenue people who will probably want to have some people there to watch the load being unloaded." Shorty said "well, that'll be fine." So Shorty headed on to Kansas City. He made it to St Louis and pulled in the big shed and got in the pick up and went to the hotel and got some rest.

He got back over there to the shed the next morning about 8 o'clock. They wasn't any sign of whiskey, the truck was unloaded. Almost all the produce was gone. Marty told him how good produce was moving and said we'll do another load next week. Marty told Shorty to just handle it with the farmers and he said he would.

Shorty left out and instead of coming back through Missouri and Cape Girardo and Arkansas he crossed the Mississippi there at St Louis went through southern Illinois and hit US 45 south through southern Illinois, Kentucky and Tennessee and into

Mississippi. He made it on back down to the scales at Tupelo Saturday morning and Dad Gum they was opened again. All his buddies were there. They asked him if he had anything on and he said no he was empty. So they told him to pull on off the scales. One of them said "Shorty we been hearing there is some mighty good moonshine down there in Alabama." "Do you recon you could get a hold of some." "Well," said Shorty "I might be able to get some." The scale man said "well if you can get us a couple of gallon." "I'll do what I can" Shorty told them. He got in his truck and headed on down the road.

Shorty got in Saturday afternoon and reported to Cracker on how everything went and then over the weekend he got with all of the farmers and told them if don't nothing happen they will want to get another load next Wednesday. Marty will send a telegram to Mr. Sam's store to let them know. That Saturday morning that Shorty was suppose to be in at Kansas City four revenuers came in there about 4 o'clock in the morning looking for the truck. A black Ford tractor with a black trailer with Alabama plates. A J.E. Thomas was driving it. They couldn't find the truck so they went in and talked to the receiver at the A&P Warehouse. He told them they were not looking for peaches or cantaloupes out of Alabama. "We got some coming from Georgia this morning but, not anything out of Alabama."

The revenuers hung around there till about 7 or 8 o'clock that morning. They decided they had some bad information. So they decided to go home for the weekend.

CHAPTER THIRTEEN

Red Turner

In the meantime, there at Garden City Cracker had a couple of guys he paid to keep their ears opened. One came to Cracker and told him the Garden City cops was suspicious of Red thought he was up to no good doing something illegal. They saw he had a pretty car riding around town spending money. As far as they knew he wasn't farming or working a job anywhere. Cracker went to talk to Red and told him not to be in town so much. Cracker said "I am going to get with my niggers and get them to haul the whiskey in boats at night on down the river." "We don't want this Memphis run to get us in trouble with the big deal in St Louis." Cracker got with Big George and Little Willie and told them what to do.

Big George said, "Mr. Cracker we can handle it but, I've got everybody about worked to death and I am going to have to have some more boys to help us." Cracker said "well don't worry about that." "Just get you a couple of niggers and send somebody with them that knows what to do and just start every week putting the Memphis whiskey on down the river."

So they started taking Red's load of whiskey on down the river about half a mile where there was a little old road that runs from the main dirt road on down to the river that nobody ever used. They got all that set-up. On Tuesday night they loaded another load of whiskey on Red for Memphis down at the new loading place. Everything went well and nothing happened so they thought everything was ok and nothing to worry about. Wednesday morning all the farmer's got their help in the field getting their produce picked and brought in to the unloading place. They got it all unloaded so about dark Big George brought his crew in and started loading the whiskey first. The watchman hollered at them and said that the old man was waving the lantern. They shut down the whiskey loading and starting working with the peaches and cantaloupes. The law came around there and sat a little bit. Then when they went on they started loading the whiskey again. The lantern started waving again so they once again they started loading the produce. This time the law came around they didn't even stop.

Shorty had told Cracker about the two gallon whiskey they needed for the scale people. Shorty said that would save them a lot of trouble with the scale people. Cracker said yea will get it for them. Shorty got Cracker to place two gallon right on the back of the truck and cover it up with hay. That way he could get it easy. So Shorty came on in and parked Cracker's truck and got in the big rig and pulled out and got on over there in Jasper and went in and got some coffee. Two or three other big rigs pulled in and got coffee. They shot the bull a little bit. When Shorty got ready to go he was parked up in the dark. He had fixed a place under the hood to put the whiskey. So he got the two gallon of whiskey out put it under the hood and headed on up the road. He got to the scales about 1:30 or 2 am in the morning. They were open, so he pulls in onto the scales. They waved him on up. They said "Shorty you're a little over on the pull wheel." Shorty said "well how much "they said "well about four cantaloupes and two gallon of whiskey if you got it." He said "yea I got it." Shorty went and pulled the hood; the scale man hollered and asked him if he had something wrong with his motor. He said "No I got this whiskey up here." "You know you can't take any chances." "If them cops in the little towns get you they try to take your license and your truck." One of them scale men said "well we know your right." "We know how they are through there." "You can't take no chances."

When Shorty got through shooting the bull with them he pulled out and eased on up there in stead of going on up 78 through Memphis like he normally would he would run he hit 45 north up into Tennennessee and Kentucky into Southern Illinois got up there and crossed the river in St Louis got in just like he did before. Dropped the truck got the pick-up went to the hotel. He came on back about 8 – 8:30 am the next morning. All the whiskey was gone except for a few watermelons. Marty told him "Man this produce is red hot." "If things goes well we will do it again next week." Shorty said "yeah we'll just plan on it and if anything happens you can let us know." So Shorty pulled out crossed the river back through southern Illinois headed on home to Alabama.

Everything was going real well in the woods with big George's crew. All the farmers were happy getting to sell their produce without having to haul it into Birmingham. Cracker was happy and Shorty was feeling pretty good. The revenuers were getting pretty tired. They had been looking and looking and hadn't found anything. And the one working Blount County and Garden City called his boss man in Birmingham and said he hadn't found nothing and looked everywhere he could think and still hadn't found nothing. And couldn't get anybody to talk and give up any information. He said "might as well give up and quit." The boss man said "no" said "Mr. Hoover wants us to keep on going." "They know there is some wildcat whiskey coming out of that area going into Memphis on up to St Louis, so we want to keep on going." So two of the revenuers got together and left one vehicle down at Arkadelphia and went in the other one with a little canoe to the bridge that crosses the Mulberry River and spent one whole day canoeing the water in the river looking all day. They would see where people had come into the river and would find maybe trot line boats tied out. They checked each one out but still couldn't find anything.

CHAPTER FOURTEEN
Red Gets Arrested

Now the Garden City police wasn't seeing Red around town like they had been and they were the ones who wanted to break the case so they got with old Judd and talked to him that they wanted him to keep an eye on Red. Wherever he saw Red they wanted him to try to find out what was going on. They told him they would keep him plenty of whiskey to drink "we won't give you too much at the time, but we will keep you in whiskey if you'll help us out." Old Judd finally decided he would. The next Tuesday night Judd was walking down the dirt road that leads from Garden City down to Arkadelphia and Red come by. It was already dark but he could tell it was Red's car. He kept easing down the road and got on there about a half a mile. It was moonlight enough where he could see the tracks where Red had turned down and went toward the river. Judd sneaked on down there and could hear something going on. He couldn't tell who was talking but he saw Red standing there with the trunk up and three guys loading something in back of the car. In the meantime, old Dan Ledbetter was out easing around and heard some noise and he sneaked down there to see what was going on. He pretty well knew what was happening. He stayed there and watched. Judd spotted him over there looking. Dan didn't see Judd. The car was loaded and they eased on out. Dan eased out ahead of Judd. Then Judd got out from there. Dan never did see Judd. The next morning Judd went straight to the police. This was making the police feel real good. They knew they were about to bust this big case. They got with the prosecuting attorney and told him what they had. They had two witnesses. Judd and old Dan Ledbetter, of course Old Dan didn't know he was going to be a witness. The prosecutor said he would talk to the judge and tell him what they had. The next day, the prosecutor went to the judge and explained to him what they had and see what he thought. He said "well it sounds pretty good, if they think they got a case just arrest him and we will set up a trial date." The next day the police went out and arrested Red. He wanted to know why they were arresting him they told him for hauling illegal whiskey. Red said, "Well I don't know where yall got that, but if I gotta go to jail then I'll go to jail." He asked how much his bond would be and they said three hundred dollars. So he opened his billfold and pulled out three hundred dollars. They let him sign his bond and released him. They gave him receipt. Red went on out of town and went to Crackers. He told him what the deal was. Cracker said we need to get you a lawyer. It doesn't need to look like I am involved in anyway. Go down to Warrior and Ray Conurff has a law office. Tell him you need a lawyer. I'll get you the money to pay for it. Talk to him and tell him you are pleading not guilty. He won't ask whether you're guilty or not. He will just handle it.

Conurff told Red that he would get in touch with the judge and the prosecuting attorney about the case for him to just go on and not worry about it. They'll have to show me what they got. I'll let them know I am representing you in the trial. So Red headed on home. The next day he and Cracker got together and decided they would hold off on hauling anymore whiskey to Memphis for awhile. Cracker got in touch with Big George the next day for him to not carry anymore whiskey to river for awhile. He didn't tell him everything but, just that they didn't want anymore arrest.

After they arrested Red the next day after he got out of jail the two Garden City cops went down to that road that Judd told them about. They parked up in the main dirt road and walked down in there. They saw where vehicles had been. They walked on a little further and could not find where there had been any whiskey there.

CHAPTER FIFTEEN
Old Dan and Judd Go to Court

Friday morning comes and the prosecuting attorney had got with the Judge and had the trail set-up for the next Friday at the City Hall in Garden City. Now the peaches, watermelons, cantaloupe deal was still going on. Cracker didn't see where that needed to stop. Everybody was notified about the trial date. Of course Red got his papers to be there. Judd got his papers and so did Old Dan Ledbetter. He was kindly puzzled he didn't really know what what was going on. They came in about 8:30 am Friday morning and got with the judge and prosecuting attorney and got everything laid out. Nine O'clock come and they all were in the room there. They stood up for the judge to come in. The prosecutor got up and read the charges against Red Turner. He said that Garden City had him for hauling illegal whiskey in the area. When they got through that part he called the first witness. It was Mr. Judd Hammock to the stand. He got up there and asked him if he was going to tell the whole truth and nothing but the truth. He said "Yes suh I'm gonna tell the truth." The prosecutor started questioning him about what he saw on a certain night down a certain dirt road in the woods. Judd started telling them about what he saw. He saw Red go down the road and he decided he would follow him. He got as close as he could without being seen. He could see them. Prosecutor asked him "Mr. Hammock what did you see then?" Judd replied "Red was standing by the car with the trunk open and three more guys it was moonlight and I am pretty sure they was black guys load something in the trunk." The prosecutor asked him if he stayed there until they finished loading and left. He said yes he stayed until they put the trunk down and the car went out. The attorney asked him if there was anything else. He said "Yes suh," said "I seed Dan Ledbetter on the other side of the road down there looking." The prosecutor said he had no further questions. Conurff got up there and started questioning Judd. Said "Judd could you identify anybody you saw down there?" Judd said "No not for sho." Said "I know it was Mr. Red's car." Conurff asked him how did it come about that he was in the area that night? So Judd told him that the Garden City police suspected Red that he was doing illegal activities and asked Judd to watch him. Conurff asked Judd if the police offered him anything for doing it. He said yes suh, theys gave me some whiskey to drink if I would help them out."

Conurff turned to the judge and said no more questions. So they let Judd be seated. And the prosecutor called Mr. Dan Ledbetter to the stand and swore him in. Asked him to tell the truth and all the truth and nothing but the truth. He said "yes sir I tell the truth." The prosecutor asked him "Mr. Ledbetter on this certain night we are talking about tell me what you observed." Dan said "I ain't seed nothing I don't know what you talking about I ain't seed nothing." Prosecutor said well "Mr. Ledbetter are you sure?" "You don't want to purge yourself." Dan said "I ain't lying I ain't lied since I stole those watermelons when I was 12 years old." "My momma whoop me so hard I ain't lied since" The policeman went over and got the prosecutors attention and said something to him. The prosecutor came back and said "Mr. Ledbetter say you haven't lied since your momma whoop you?" Old Dan said "no suh I ain't lying," the prosecutor said "well what about these times the police caught you drunk and carried you in and put you in jail you claim you ain't drunk.?" Old Dan said "well those boys ain't never seen me really drunk." The prosecutor said "well Mr. Ledbetter we got a witness that says you was there and saw you down there and saw you down there watching." Old Dan said "I ain't seed nothing." The prosecutor said "well so you're going to tell me you didn't see Judd down there and he was watching the same thing you was watching." Old Dan said "I seed him." Prosecutor says, "Oh so now you're going to tell me that you did see Mr. Turner and three other men down there loading something presumed to be wildcat whiskey into the trunk of a car." Old Dan said "I ain't seed nothing" and pointed to Judd and said "I seed him when he thought he seed me saw him." Prosecutor turned around and scratched his head, pulled his britches out of the crack of his butt and looked at the judge and said "Your Honor there will be no more questions." The judge picks up the hammer bam bam bam on the table and said Dismissed!

CHAPTER SIXTEEN

Jesse Taylor

Cracker Black didn't go to the trial. He knew about it but didn't go. He didn't want anyone to think he was interested in it so he didn't go. When Red Turner got out he thought Man that was close. I am going to have to be careful. He went out of town in the opposite direction. He wanted to go see Cracker but, he figured they were watching him so he made a loop around town and then made his way to Cracker's house. Cracker happened to be home. He asked him how did everything come out and Red said "well it came out fine" "They didn't find me guilty." Cracker said "well we going to move that loading place on down the river about a half a mile so there's not a road that goes from the Arkadelphia road to the river." "On the night that your going to load we'll have the niggers down there to have it next to the edge of the road so when you come by they can have you loaded in about three minutes and you'll be gone." Red said "Cracker that part sounds good but, I got something else on my mind." Cracker said "what is it?" "Red said, "Well every time I go through Jasper, them police have really been eyeing me heavy." "Every night they follow me out of town." "It's just a matter of time before they going to stop me." "They'll have me or either I'll have to run off and leave my car." "And then they'll catch me when they find out whose car it is." Cracker said "we'll let me see, my main man in Memphis has already talked about switching cars he got a long 41 Buick." "This next trip leave your car up there and come home in his car." Red said "well that sounds good but, I am really worried about this next trip." "They really been keeping an eye on me." Cracker said "do you know where Jesse Taylor lives?" Red said "yea I know where Jesse Taylor lives." Cracker said "well does he still have that hotrod 41 Chevrolet pick-up?" Red said "well yea as far as I know he still got it." "Well get him to come see me tonight." Red said "yea." Cracker said "this is what we'll do, is I'll get him to go over there and run interference." "I know he is a hot-rodder and drives fast." "Well let him go over there and get the law after him and then you can go on through there." Red said "yea that sounds like it will work."

So Red left and went on to hunt up Jesse and told him that Cracker wanted to talk to him. So late that afternoon Jesse went down to Cracker's house. He and Cracker went out to the barn and Cracker asked him how everything was going asked about the family and everything. Jesse said "well everything been going good." "I been helping daddy on the farm and everything's going good." Cracker said "well you want to make a little extra money? "Jesse said "Yeah as a matter of fact I would." So Cracker outlined everything and let him know what they had in mind. So Jesse said "yeah I'll do it." Cracker said "I'll give you 50 dollars and if you get caught I'll pay the fine." Jesse said "Man you can't beat that." Cracker said "tomorrow night we gonna run a load so we all need to get together and get everything planned out"

So the next morning they got together and got everything set up where Red would meet and Red would get behind Jesse. Cracker said "well you boys know them roads over there better than I do so I don't want to tell you how to do it." Jesse said "yeah my daddy used to work in them coal mines over there and I ran them roads a lot." "I know all the back roads." Cracker said "well you and Red talk it over and see how ya'll want to do it."

So they did and Jesse asked Red if he knew where this certain off road was before you get into Jasper. Red said "yeah I know where that's at." Jesse said "what we'll do is we will get together between the loading place and Arkadelphia." "I'll run a little ways in front of you and we'll run on over to that road and I'll stop and make sure you get placed right and I'll go into town and get them stirred up." "When you see me come back out with them behind me all you have to do is pull out and you'll be clear sailing." Jesse asked Red if he knew where that little pull off road right before you cross the big creek before you get to Arkadelphia and Red said yeah. Jesse said "well what time you going out tonight?" "You are going tonight right?" Red said "yeah I am going." Jesse said "well what time do you think you'll be loaded up and headed out?" Red said "well I want to be loaded up by 9 o'clock and headed that away." Jesse said "I'll tell you what I am going to do, I'll be setting right inside that road when you come by, and I'll pull out behind you." "In a little bit I'll pass you then you can follow me on to the parking place."

CHAPTER SEVENTEEN
Momma Pearl

With plans made Jesse went on back home to take care of a few things he had to do at the house. About four o'clock that evening his momma, which her name was Pearl Taylor. She said "Jesse I been wanting to go over and see Aunt Irene" which was her sister. "Jesse I want you to run me over to there." Jesse said "well I guess I can I can't stay long I got some plans for tonight." She said "well don't worry we won't be over there long so they loaded up and headed over to Aunt Irene's." It was about four miles away winding on the dirt road through them hills. So they got over there and Pearl and Irene got busy talking and catching up on all the gossip. It was getting pretty late and Jesse said, "Momma" said "come on you know I've got to go." "I got plans tonight." Pearl said "we'll go just in a little bit." So it rocked on and before Jesse knew it it had done got dark. He said "Momma!" "I've got somewhere I got to be at 8 o'clock you just stay here at Aunt Irene's and about 10 I'll come back and pick you up." His momma said "naw I'll just go with you." He said "momma I ain't got time to carry you by home." She said "naw I'll just go with ye." He said "Now Momma!" "I don't want you to go with me." "You just stay here at Aunt Irene's and I'll come back here and pick you up." She said "Now Jesse I said I'd go with you."

Pearl weighed about 300 lbs so Jesse wasn't going to do too much arguing. So Jesse said "well come on." So Pearl loaded up and they took off. Headed for the road right before you get to the creek where they was supposed to pull in behind Red after they get the whiskey loaded. So while they was sitting down there Jesse decided he ought to tip his momma off and let her know what they were going to do. She said "Good! That'll be fun said I like to ride fast and have fun." She looked over at Jesse and said "Jesse you got anything?" He said "Momma I just got a little bit in a vanilla flavoring bottle in the glove box." "But momma I can't be dranking and drive." She said "you drive I'll drank." So she got that about a quarter of a pint of moonshine in the flavoring bottle. She got to drinking and feeling pretty good. Finally Red came by and they pulled out behind him and on down a ways where there was a good straight away Jesse passed him.

Red and Jesse got up there at the parking place and stopped, got out of the vehicles. Jesse said "Red you just back right up in there" said "nobody apt to use this road." "Don't nobody hardly ever use this road so when you see me and the law comes back by here we'll be headed south and you'll be headed north." Red said "yeah go on and do whatever it is you got to do." So Jesse and big momma headed on into town and they come in there at the first red light. Jesse spotted the law setting right down there on the side of the street. Instead of going on right down there by them he took a left and made a block and when he came out by them he shot the juice to it and turned a tale spin. Burning rubber and Pearl was hollering "Woo Hoo!" "Woo Hoo!". The law turned their light on and pulled out behind them. Here they come hard as they could go down 78 highway probably running 70 mile an hour. When Red saw them go by he let them get on by and then he eased out. Everything went real smooth with him. Jesse was headed down there to a road that went way back over toward Cordova. It was dirt road so he thought he could dust them out and get away from them. He headed out and the law was pretty close behind him. What Jesse didn't know was that about 3 mile there was a bridge out. Jesse didn't know this but, the law did. After he had gone passed a road he could have cut off they backed off and didn't want to take a chance on wrecking. Jesse got on over there about half a mile he saw a sign that said bridge out. He said "Man oh Man." His momma was still carrying on and having a big time so he decided to run on over there and be sure. Sure enough it was out so he decided to turn around and come back a few hundred yards there was a little side road so he turned off into it. Hoping the law would go on by. He was hoping he could get away from them. The law was looking for him everywhere. They come along and spotted him up in that little road. They turned in there and blocked him in and jumped out demanding he get out of the truck. They told him to put his hands up. They took his identification and found out who he was. They hand cuffed him to the door of the car. They were raising cane. So far Pearl had sat in the truck and had not said anything. They started questioning Jesse. They said "Jesse what in the world were you doing?" Jesse replied, "Aw nothing, you know I just like to drive fast and have fun." They said "Naw you was up to something." "You came right in there where we was at and provoked us" He said "Naw I just like to drive fast." One of the cops said "Well Jesse you going to jail." Jesse said "well if I have to go to jail I'll just go to jail." "I just like to drive fast." About that time Pearl got out of the truck and walked around there she told that cop, she was pretty high by this time, "Ain't nobody going to jail." The cop said "yes ma am Jesse's going to jail." She had a big old pocket book with about a foot and half handles on it she swung that thing and cold cocked that cop up side the head and knocked him down just about out. She drug him back over there away from the truck and sat down on him holding him down. He finally came to and was trying to get up he couldn't get up because she was sitting on him. The other cop ran back over to the car and got on the little ol radio hollering "Officer down! Officer down!" Another set of cops in Carbon Hill heard the call and came back to him on the radio. He wanted to know what the trouble was. He responded by saying officer down officer down. The other cop wanted to know his location. He said about 2 mile off of 78 hwy and boy here those two cops come wide open. In the meantime the Jasper cop got up his nerve and came up there to try and rescue his buddy and Ms Taylor cold cocked him and piled him on top of the other one. She sat down on them both riding them like a hoss. Hollering Woo hoo!" "Woo hoo!". About that time the Carbon Hill cops got there flying in sideways with there lights a flashing and siren a whining. They jumped out with their pistols. Ms Taylor grabbed the cop on top of the pile and twisted his arm back behind him and said "Holler calf rope." Well he hollered calf rope. She said "tell them policeman to back off." He wouldn't do it so she grabbed that arm tighter and twisted it tighter. He hollered "guys back off she's killing me boys, she's killing me. They holstered their guns and went back down to the car. Jesse said "let me handle this. Let me talk to momma." Said "you got my license, you got my identification, you know who I am, you know what kind of truck I got said I am going to try to talk momma into letting me take her home." "I'll come back over here tomorrow and whatever I have to do pay a fine, or go to jail." At first the police didn't much want to do it. Then he looked around there at momma and said "ok Jesse tell her to let me up and I'll unlock you from the truck." She let him up and finally agreed to go along with it. Jesse said "how much will the fine be?" He said "forty dollars and twenty dollars court cost." Ms Taylor turned around and looked him straight in the eye and he said "No No it will be twenty dollars and five dollars court cost." She was satisfied with that. So the policeman was real nice to her and helped her into the truck and said "Now Ms. Taylor you just settle down and Jesse's going carry you home, now just settle down and everything will be alright". So Jesse got his momma and headed on home with her. Pearl said "Jesse this was fun let's do it again." Jesse said "Now momma."

CHAPTER EIGHTEEN
Day After the Ride

The next morning before Jesse could go over to Jasper he had to hunt up Cracker and get his fine money. He finally found him and told him what happened. Cracker asked if everything went alright with Red. He said "Oh yeah everything went fine with Red." He told him what the fine was going to cost. Cracker said "well I'm going to go ahead and give you your fifty, twenty for the fine and five for the court cost." "Son, you go ahead and get paid off and everything." "You know we might need to use you again." Jesse said "yeah just let me know if you need me."

In the meantime, everything was going pretty smooth around Garden City. They finally got electricity and some of the main businesses like Mr. Sam's store got a telephone. The other stores some of them got phones. Of course the police department and the sheriff department got one. Hayden, Blount Springs, Bangor and Garden City all around got telephones so communications was better. Everything was going pretty smooth in the woods. Little Willie and Big George was making whiskey. Little Ben was going everywhere with Mr. Sam every time he had to make a trip. Once a week Mr. Sam would carry Little Ben down to the Mulberry river fishing. They was just as tight as they could be.

The church got its pretty chandeliers like it wanted. It had made up enough money to get some real pretty lights. Mr. Sam was still getting in lots of sugar that they would need for the whiskey operation. Meanwhile, over on Oak Grove Mountain the Swan's lived on one side of the big holler and the Thomas' lived on the other side. There was a big hole of water that they all like to swim in called the "Blue hole." That morning the Swan girls had been gathering cantaloupes for a man out of the Carolinas, he was coming for a load that evening. The Thomas boys had been picking peaches and getting them ready to send to town. That afternoon they were over in a little field called the five acre field. They had set out some tomatoes. The biggest boys were over there hoeing the tomatoes and Harold the oldest was plowing the tomatoes. The twins were ripping and romping through the woods. The Swan girls decided they would go to the blue hole a swimming. The twins saw where they were going and came back a hollering the Swan girls are a heading for the blue hole. Boy they throwed their hoes down and took off. Now Harold the oldest was out at the end cooling the mule and drinking some water. The other boys came running by him wide open. He said "hold it hold it!" "Where do you think you are going?"

They said the Swan girls were at the blue hole and we're going up there to go a swimming. Harold said "well I'll tell you what, daddy said we better get this field finished before we come in for supper." "I'll give you 45 minutes." "In 45 minutes you better be back with the hoe in our hand." So they all agreed and took off running. Everybody back in them days probably swam naked if there weren't any boys where the girls were and girls where the boys were. If it was mixed that just swam in there clothes. Those boys took them about ten minutes to get to the blue hole and they came off that hill hollering and yipping. They jumped in swimming around getting cooled off and the little twin Swan boy was sitting up on the hill. He took off over to the field where his daddy was and yelled "Daddy Daddy the girls are in the blue hole a swimming and the Thomas boys came over." His daddy said "son you go back and tell them girls they better be at the barn in thirty minutes." "The man from the Carolina's will be there for the cantaloupes."

Everybody was having a big time a swimming. Oldest boys and the oldest girls all paired off. The boys were all trying to get some sugar or whatever and the girls slapping them saying stopped that we are cousins. The little Thomas twins and the little Swan twins were sitting on the side dangling their feet in the water. One of the Thomas twins looked over at the little Swan Twin girl and said "are we cousins?" She said "I reckon. "They all stayed as long as they could without getting in trouble. Then they all headed back to hoeing and loading the cantaloupes.

CHAPTER NINETEEN
Securing the Load

Shorty was in St Louis already unloaded on Friday morning. Marty was paying Shorty for the produce to get headed back to Alabama. Marty asked him was there any tomatoes down there. Shorty said "yeah they some tomatoes growing around there." Marty said "if they good man I could use bout 50 or so crates on that next load." "There red hot right now." "Peaches and tomatoes are red hot." "Cantaloupes is pretty good and watermelons is good." "If you need be cut back on the watermelons to get the tomatoes on that is fine." "See what you can do." Shorty said "yeah I'll see what we can do."

So Shorty come on back home and went to see Mr. General. He said "Marty wants some good tomatoes and I knew you would know more about who had them then I would." General said "yeah there two or three good tomato growers up on Hog Mountain." "I'll run up there tomorrow and see what I can find out." "Marty said he could stand about 5.25 a crate." General said "well I'll see if we can get them for that." "Are you going to have to cut back on something to get them on the truck?" And Shorty said "yeah we going to have to cut back on watermelons and cantaloupes maybe a few." General said "Now Shorty you know I know about trucking and that truck ought to haul about 75

crates of tomatoes and still the same amount you been hauling."
Shorty had to think fast, he said "well you know how they are up
there in Mississippi, and Arkansas." "I don't want to get up there
and be overloaded." General said "yeah you're right."

Next morning General headed up to Hog Mountain. He made
a deal with the Green's and the Johnson's to have about 30 crates
a piece ready for the next Wednesday. He made a deal that he
would pick them up on his truck and pay them about 4.00 a crate.
That way he made about a 1.00 per crate. The deal was settled.
Mr. General had his own ideas from where they were loading the
produce and who was handling it but, he wasn't involved in it so
he wasn't going to worry about it. From his side of things it was
a good deal. He got to sell his produce and earn an honest wage.
Now Ms Pauline on the other hand had heard a little bit of low
talk that there might be a little bit of moonshine whiskey being
hauled with those loads. When Mr. General came in that night
she said "General there's a little bit of talk that there might be
some wild cat whiskey being hauled with those loads and I don't
want us to be involved with nothing like that." General said "well
Pauline I don't know anything don't want to know anything."
"We're selling peaches and tomatoes that's all I know."

Revenuer Still On the Trail

Back to the loading place in Garden City where they load the whiskey first and then put the produce on top of it, everything had been going pretty good. They had one nigger that his job was to watch the window and he would tell George what was going on. When he alerted George to the signal any moving of the whiskey was stopped and the only loading was the peaches and cantaloupes etc. On the next load that was lined up they had the produce ready and the whiskey. The Garden City Police came around and just started hanging around. They wouldn't leave. They hung around about an hour. Cracker got a hold of a nigger and told him to slip up the railroad about a half of mile. There's a lot of brush piled up. You got any matches he said Yes suh. Well you go up there and catch that brush pile on fire and then slip back down the railroad and come on back. It's dark so nobody will see you. So he slipped on up there and started the fire. In about ten minutes the fire was burning big and a lot of smoke so the police left and went up there. The volunteer fire department was there and about half the town. So this created a diversion to they could go back to their loading without any trouble. All the whiskey and produce got loaded and everything went fine.

Now Cracker and Big George had seen a time or two the

car that the revenuer had been driving. Cracker still felt pretty safe. The revenuer had been looking about a month or two and still hadn't found anything. Now one morning the revenuer had parked his car all the way down at Blount Springs by the railroad tracks. He had walked the woods and walked any little trail and had not found anything. So this particle morning he parked way down there. He started walking again and still had not found anything until about 3:00 that afternoon he ran up on this good trail that went off the railroad track. He found the wreckage of the push buggy that had gotten beat up in the crash. He thought to himself, well I might be on to something here. He got off the trail about a hundred yards. Every now and then he would get back on the trail to make sure he was going in the right direction. The look out man on the bluff with the mirror, every morning when they would really get to working Big George would have him signal just to test that everything was working. If they received anymore signal that day they knew it was something. The lookout man on the bluff he saw some movement on the side of the hill about 300 or 400 hundred yards before you got to the vats. He watched real close until he finally made out that it was a man. A white man! So he got his mirror and started flashing them about 200 hundred yards down there where they was. Big George got the message and said Little Willy you come with me and told the rest to scatter in the woods. If they find the whiskey they'll just find the whiskey but we don't want anybody to get caught. He told Little Willy to follow him. So they made a circle to left and back over the hill. They hid down between two big rocks. They were just watching. About that time the revenuer came by where they were hid and Big George jumped out on him and threw him on the ground. Don't really know exactly what happened, we just know that the revenuer never found anything and some of the other black people who were working the vats saw Little Willy and Big

George dragging a couple of Croker sacks around to the vat. Looked like something red dripping out of the bottom. Big George throwed his sack in one vat and Little Willy put his in the other.

CHAPTER TWENTY-ONE
Nobody Knows for Sure

At this point nobody really knew what happened except them but, Big George got to thinking he ought to tell Cracker what happened. That night Big George and Little Willey headed over to Cracker's. They caught up with him at the house. They went for a ride down the road a little way and Cracker said "what you got on your mind Big George?" "You look pretty serious" Big George told him everything that happened. Cracker said "Dam, this could get serious." Big George said "yes suh." Cracker asked him if any of the other niggers knew what happened. George said "Nah Suh just me and Willey that's all." Cracker said "that's good." "We got to find his car." "He parked somewhere so we got to find his car tonight." They left George's car at Crackers and got in Crackers pick-up. They started riding all the little roads and crossroads. They finally found it on a little road close to the tunnel that goes to Hoss Mountain. He had parked down there and started out walking. Cracker said "we got to do something with this car." So Cracker found the key under the seat and told Big George to get in it and follow him and Little Willey. So they headed down through Hayden, down some back roads through Niota, Alabama now close to Trafford. The road went right by a big cliff that dropped down into the Warrior River. It was deep water there. So they shoved it off into the Warrior River. Cracker told them that it is apt to not be found for a long time. We had to get it away from up there where it was.

They all went back home. Cracker said "so far we shouldn't have nothing to worry about." "You just carry the operation on just like before." "Nobody knows nothing but you and Willey." So the next morning Cracker got into his old pick-up and headed over to 78 hwy to Hollis' joint. He went in talking to him and they went in to Hollis' office. Cracker outlined what had happened. Bill Hollis said "Dammit to hell, this thing has gotten big." Cracker said "yeah, but so far we don't have anything to worry about but, we are where we're at." "And we got to go on." "I got some things I got in mind doing," Bill asked him what it was. Cracker said "well you heard of Bangor cave?" Bill said "yeah I know about Bangor Cave." "Well it's about 4 miles down the railroad from Garden City." "The railroad runs about 75/ 85 yards from the mouth of the cave." "We can still use the railroad to carry all our sugar and jugs to the cave" "I am going to set-up a still in the cave." "I will put a man with it." "If things get too hot, you know I got my men around watching and listening; I can get word to them and leak out to the law that there is a big moonshine still operating in Bangor Cave." "Then the law can come in and bust it up." "It'll take the heat off the other operation." Said "we will let them find some whiskey and catch somebody." Bill said "Man we can't let them find much whiskey can we?" Cracker said "yeah we got let them find about 75 or a hundred gallon." "If they don't find any whiskey they won't stop looking." "Let them feel good about what they've done." Bill said "yeah, but what about this letting them catch somebody?" Cracker said "I got this black guy named Ely Merrell." "I can put him down there." "Not just to get caught but, if he does he won't talk." Hollis said "Man you don't know what they'll do to him to make him talk." "I don't like that idea at all." Cracker said "well he's 51 years old and he hadn't ever said a word in his life."

CHAPTER TWENTY-TWO
Bangor Cave

Bangor Cave was a big cave had three front rooms, like three auditoriums. In the twenties and early thirties, it was an underground casino, dancehall, and whorehouse, just whatever went in there. They said that the likes of John Dillinger out of Chicago, hid out in there. Bangor was a thriving town back in those days. It had hotels and stores. In the thirties the cave got burnt out and after that it went down to nothing. It has been sitting there ever since.

Bill said "Cracker go on and do whatever you're going to do." Cracker said "well I never intended for it to get this big, but I guess we will just have to live with it, but" said "as long nobody don't talk so there's no way to trace it back to me or you either one." With that Cracker went on back home and got busy everything lined up to get the equipment to Bangor Cave to build the still. He got to thinking about methane gas being in the cave. He sure wouldn't want to start the still and it blow up and kill somebody. So he remembered this guy that had been a coal miner all his life that lived over toward Empire.

He had known him along time. More or less a casual acquaintance, but still knew him.

This guy worked at night and was home in the daytime. His

name was Delton Franklin. So Cracker headed out to see him. He told him a little about what was going on. This was all being kept to himself so he told him that he just wanted to make a little moonshine in the cave. He just wanted to make sure it wouldn't blow up and hurt somebody. Make sure there's no danger. Delton told him that yeah he would come over there this evening. Cracker said "well good." "Just meet me this evening over at Bangor and we will go over there together." Cracker said "I'll pay you for it." Delton said "Nah just give me about 5 gallon," Cracker said "well I'll buy you 10 gallons of gas." Delton said, "Cracker I said 5 gallon I am not worried about no gas." Cracker caught on and said "Oh well yeah I can handle that." So they met that evening and went and checked the cave out.

Franklin told him that he had run two or three little test that they run in the mine. He didn't see any sign of methane gas. So they got ready to leave and Cracker told Delton. "I'll be over that way in a few days with your whiskey. ""If you happen to not be there or either asleep one I'll just put it out there in the barn loft." Delton said well that will be fine.

General, Brady and Lorene

General and Brady

General Thomas & Sons

Seven Sons

The twins, Terry & Kerry

Nine sons

Ten Sons

Pauline and General

FBI Alerted

Cracker rushed everybody up to get that still ready. He wanted to turn the law loose on it. That agent usually called in at least every three days to the Birmingham office. By this time it had been about five or six days since they heard from him and were beginning to get a little worried about him. After it had been eight days the Birmingham office called Washington. The guy they talked to at the FBI in Washington said that this didn't sound good. He better turn this over to Hoover there in Washington. So he got J Edgar Hoover on the line. He was the head of the FBI. The man from Birmingham told him he hadn't heard from the agent in about eight days which was unlike this man not to call in. Hoover said if he hasn't checked in or called in two more days call me back. In a couple more days went by and they hadn't heard a thing from the agent working Blount County. The head man from Birmingham called Hoover back and said Man there is no sign of him. Something is just not right. Hoover told him he would call him back.

Big Jim Folsom was the governor of Alabama. A tall man about six feet eight inches tall. Hoover told his secretary to get the Governor on the phone. The secretary called the Governor and got him on the line. She said this is the FBI in Washington

Mr. Hoover wants to talk to you. The Governor responded OK. J Edgar got on the line with Big Jim. Hoover said "Jim I got an agent missing down there in Blount County." "There's a lot of whiskey being run out of there to Memphis and St Louis." "He was working that case and hasn't checked in with Birmingham in ten days." Jim said "Edgar" Said "I believe everything will be alright." "You know I'm from up there in Cullman County." "I know all those old boys up there." Now there are probably some making a little dranking whiskey but, they ain't nothing big like that going on up there." Hoover said "well if my agent doesn't show up in a few days you better use your state men and get the sheriff up there to looking." "If we haven't found him in five or six days we are going to swarm that place with federal agents." "We are going to find out what's going on down there." Big Jim said "I'll check into it and see what is happening."

A couple of more days they was going to ship out another load of whiskey to St Louis. Big George told Cracker said "we ain't got but about half of the load we got going." Big George said "I guess I can run off a couple of these vats and have enough to load." Cracker said "yeah that's what we need to do." "We sure do not want to miss this load." So George ran off two vats. In fact it was the two vats they had thrown the two sacks in. He got the whiskey ran out and all the mesh out and burnt.

So all the farmers got their produce over there to load. General had the tomatoes and everything. Had the whiskey in the woods behind where the dock was. Everything got loaded seemed to be going fine. Shorty came and picked up the load as usual. The scale men wanted some more of the whiskey so Shorty had pulled out a couple of jugs from that shipment and put it under the hood in the secret hiding place. He got over there to the scales and talked to the guys. He was alright on his weight. He gives them their whiskey and headed on toward St Louis. He was running a little bit late it was getting to be about 9 o'clock in the morning. In the meantime, Big Jim called Ed Miller the sheriff of Blount

County that he had heard from J Edgar Hoover from the FBI in Washington about the missing agent. He wanted Ed to see what he could find out about him. Ed told big Jim we will get my men out and ease around and see what we can find out. For all we know that man could be in St Louis by now. About the time the sheriff said that Shorty came up over a little hill and read a sign that said St Louis 30 miles.

Shorty got on into the market and headed to the hotel. He rested and came on back over the next morning. The tomatoes and peaches well everything was selling red hot. Marty told him that morning to do another load next Wednesday. Have it here by Thursday evening so I will have it to sell on Friday morning. Be sure and tell your brother to get me some more of those good tomatoes. Shorty said "yeah I think we can handle it." So Shorty headed on back home down through Illinois and way in the night he got to the scales in Mississippi. They wanted to know if he had anything on and he said "no I'm empty." So they told him to pull off over there. So he got out and was talking to them. One of the scale men said "Shorty that was the best whiskey I ever had in my life." "Seemed like it was sort of sweet." Shorty laughed and said "they might have used a little bit more sugar in this run."

CHAPTER TWENTY-FOUR
Decoy

Cracker got all the equipment down to Bangor and got that pot kicked off. He got Ely Merrell to watch it. When he needed help he would send him help. The first run off they just kept in the cave if they didn't need it. After that if they needed the run off they would use it for the St Louis or Memphis run, but if they didn't need it they just kept it there. Everything was going real good.

In the meantime, Mr. Acton over in Acton Bend had a real good early cotton patch. The cotton was coming in real good and it was getting to be a few days over into September. The cotton was opening real good. Back then they would pick it twice sometimes three times. When it got fairly white they would pick it once and then would wait till it opened all the way to pick it again. This was so if they had bad weather it would not ruin the quality of the cotton. Mr. Acton had gotten him up a crew of whites and blacks to pick. James was helping pick and then help weigh. One morning this big old black lady was picking cotton and a black girl called Sister Gal. She was about 16 years old. She and James was picking along side of Liza. All morning long she noticed they were getting a little bit chummy. About that afternoon after the first weighing up they started falling way behind Liza. She looked back and could see they were getting really chummy with each other. Long after while, they were about 40 yards back behind her in that tall cotton she would have to stand up to see. She looked back and did not see them. She pulled her sack off of her neck and walked back there. She found their sacks but they were gone. Old Liza says Hmm, Uh Uh Uh. She went on back to picking cotton she looked back again and saw they was back picking. She just shook her head and said Hmm, Hmm, Hmm. This was the last weighing up. They had quit about 5:30 to weigh. Big tall James got up on the wagon. Mr Acton started weighing his cotton, James usually pick 45-55 pound to the weighing up. This time he didn't have but 25 pounds. His daddy said "James what's the problem?" "This ain't near the cotton you usually pick." James said "Daddy I was feeling bad this evening." He went on to weighing. About this time they were weighing Sister Gal's cotton. She usually picked about 35 pounds to the weighing up but she had 58 pounds. Mr. Acton said "Sister Gal really got on the ball she picked a lot of cotton." James said "she must have been feeling good." Old Liza said ah huh ahhh huhhhh.

CHAPTER TWENTY-FIVE
The Baptism

Now the only churches around Garden City was the white Baptist church and the black Baptist church down at the edge of town. The white preacher Adams and preacher Hudson the black preacher they had talked in the summer about maybe having a revival and maybe having it together. Because most of the time when the blacks had a revival quite a few whites would go and when the whites had theirs a several blacks would go. They had been talking about having it together maybe in September. They had been bringing up before their congregations and it seemed alright by everybody so they set their meeting on the third Saturday in September. Since they already had electricity at the white church, the black church was about to get it, but since it was already at the white church they decided to go on and have it there.

So they started getting the word out about when the revival was going to be. They got the word out around Bangor and up at Hanceville so they would have a big meeting. The white pastor Bro Adams would preach the first night and then Bro Hudson would preach the second night. They decided to run six nights so each one would have three nights a piece. So on the first night of the revival Bro Adams was preaching that night. They had a big crowd that night. Some had come in their cars and some in their trucks. They also had some come in their mule and wagon. Some people just walked over to the church. Back then when people lived four or five miles away they would load their trucks up and come to the revival. They had so many people there they couldn't all get in the house. They had the windows up and it was a little cool outside but it hadn't turned off cold yet, so people had their heads in the window. Some of this was because they couldn't get in the church house and some of it was because that was as close as they wanted to get. A lot of people wanted to be close enough to hear but didn't want to be too close because they didn't want to do anything about the situation. That night about three came down the aisle and got saved that night. Everybody was happy and seemed like it was getting off to a good start.

On the next night Bro Hudson was preaching and was really turning it on. They had a real good singing and then came the preaching time. Man he really laid it on them. The whites and the blacks was really getting into the service clapping their hands and shouting "Say That!" "Amen Bro Hudson!" "Preach Brother!" They were just having themselves a good time in the spirit. As the service was coming to a close and the last song had been sang they was giving the altar call for people to come down and reunite themselves with the church or either come down for salvation. There was about six that made the move that night. The choir began to sing with that good old black gospel harmony singing Victory in Jesus and everyone was singing, shouting, and crying just having a good time in the spirit.

On the third night it was Bro Adams time again even though the spirit might not have been as hot as the 2nd night but, his message was strong and everybody was really moved by the word. That night there was four that came down. It was a black boy, a black girl, a white boy, and a white girl. That brought everybody together that night. This time everybody was singing blacks and whites "Just a little Talk with Jesus" and praising the Lord.

Well the Brimley boys that lived about five miles down the Mulberry River below Garden City heard about the revival. They didn't really hate niggers but, they didn't like the idea of the two churches having revival together. They decided the fourth night they was going to go and have some fun. That was the night for Bro Hudson to preach. So they had the singing and the testimony service before the preaching. Bro Hudson got up to preach and man did he really burn the timbers that night. His message was on the second coming of Christ and he preached a real good sermon and everyone was listening intensely even those that had their head stuck in the window listening. The Brimley boys had already decided they was going to interrupt the service that night by throwing some big rocks up on the tin roof. They had no idea what he was going to preach on that night. Bro Hudson was getting down to the end of the service and told them "Jesus is going to come back, when you least expect it." Crowd, "That's Right." Bro Hudson, "And I say it, I say to you it will be a time when you think not." "Like a thief in the night." Crowd "Amen Bro Hudson" Bro Hudson, "With a great noise He will make his return." And about that time about three big rocks hit on top of the church house. Wham, Bam, Bam, sounded like thunder. You could have heard a pin drop it got so quiet in there. About five decided they better run on down to the altar sweating and hearts beating fast. They decided it was about time they get saved just in case. Things got settled down and Bro Hudson finished up his sermon and in all about seven people got saved that night.

On the fifth night it was Bro Adams turn. Everything was made ready. The church came together and sang and gave their testimony in the service. Bro Adams got started preaching. Well the Brimley Brothers, three of them 14, 16, and 17. They weren't really all that mean just mischievous. They had decided they were going to do it again. Deacon Brown however, had gotten with two or three young boys to stand around on the edge in the dark and see if they could tell what was going on out there. He wanted them to catch whoever was doing it. When the service was about to close that night they did it again. The rock hit the top of the church Wham Bam Bam and this time rattled the windows making a lot of racket. The boys that were looking out saw them. They took out after the Brimley boys. They caught the two youngest and brought them back to the church. They got the deacons to come out and talk to them. They knew these boys momma and daddy. They told them "we could have you put in jail, but we don't want to do that." "If y'all will tell your brother that got away to come tomorrow night and come in and listen to the sermon we will act like this never happened." So they went home and got with their brother. He didn't really want to do it but they knew they might go to jail and then their momma and daddy would have found out so they all decided they would go to revival the next night.

Friday night rolled around this was Bro Hudson's night to preach. Saturday was the sixth night. They had a real big crowd. I guess it was the biggest crowd of all. The service was real good. There were lots of good spiritual singing and testifying. Everybody was really getting into the service. Then it came time for the preaching. Bro Hudson's message that night was on forgiveness. The big theme was forgiveness and that we should forgive each other. He brought it around that is how we get saved is that Jesus died on the cross for us and He forgives us of all of our sins. It seemed to go over well and five went forward at the altar call. Two of the Brimley boys went down and then finally the oldest one went down. After the service they always gave everybody a chance to tell why they went forward whether it was for salvation or reuniting with the church. They got to the two Brimley boys and they said they got saved and then the oldest said he had been saved and he had backslide and that he was sorry he had talked his younger brother into throwing the rocks on top of the church. Everybody forgave them and shook their hands and hugged necks. That brought the revival to an end of the six night revival.

Deacons from both churches and the preachers from both churches got together and decided they would have their baptizing on the next Sunday afternoon after church. They wound up with 23 converts that had gotten saved and they wound up with 13 backsliders that had come back. About three of them backsliders decided they wanted to get re-baptized so they wound up with 26 to be baptized that Sunday.

The next Sunday afternoon rolled around and church service was over. Everybody hurried home to get something to eat before the baptism. It was going to be at 2:00 but about 1:00 many started coming in to the baptizing hole. They had a good hole that stayed full even when the river was down that was about chest deep. They all got assembled on the bank. The preachers had sticks in their hands so they could walk steady out into the river. They were looking for a good spot in the hole to baptize in. So the singing started on the banks. There were lots of people out that day. They sang a few old hymns and then they started into singing "Shall we gather at the river, where bright angel feet have trod, with its crystal tide forever flowing by the throne of God? Yes, we'll gather at the river, the beautiful, and the beautiful river; Gather with the saints at the river that flows by the throne of God. On the margin of the river, washing up its silver spray, we will talk and worship ever, all the happy golden day. Ere we reach the shining river, Lay we every burden down; Grace our spirits will deliver, and provide a robe and crown. At the smiling of the river, Mirror of the Savior's face, Saints, whom death will never sever, lift their songs of saving grace. Soon we'll reach the silver river, Soon our pilgrimage will cease; soon our happy hearts will quiver with the melody of peace." This song could be heard for miles around. The rich voices beautiful blending of the blacks and the whites singing in perfect harmony.

After they finished that song they had a prayer. Then they lined up in two lines. One was for Preacher Adams and the other was for Preacher Hudson. They would baptize one at a time each preacher taking their turn. They baptized in the name of the Father, the Son, and the Holy Ghost. When they got to the last one that finished up their service and everyone returned home. Many people watched from the woods that day especially Big George and Little Willie. They sure was hoping that there wasn't anybody being raised from the dead that day. Little Willie looked at Big George and said, "I sho am glad they got it did." Big George just looked at Little Willie and shook his head saying "Willie we gots work to do."

CHAPTER TWENTY-SIX
Goin Good

Everything was going good with Big George in the woods. Everything was going good for the cave operation. They were keeping the supplies to Ely. So everything was running smooth. They had gotten out another load on that 41 Buick for Memphis. Shorty got into St Louis with that load and everything as usual it went real good. Shorty told Marty that the watermelon man said he was getting slack on melons was there anything else he could use. Marty said "yeah I can use some turnip greens." Shorty said "well, it's a little early for fall greens but I can see what I can do."

Before Shorty left he said "if we can't get watermelons and we can get greens how many can you use?" Marty said "at least a hundred bushel of the cut greens with ice." "I can pay at least 2.75 a bushel." Shorty said "we will see what we can do." So Shorty headed on back to Alabama. A couple of loads of that shine had got into Memphis. One old nigger went into a shot house and dranked him two or three shots he got up and said that is the best moonshine I ever drank in my life it had a little sweet taste. The old lady running the shot house said "Yeah I's think theys using a little more sugar then they use to."

On the way back to Alabama the scale boys over there in

Mississippi ordered a couple of more gallons of whiskey. Shorty told them he didn't think it would be any problem. He would try to get to them some. So Shorty got on back in home and went to see General about turnip greens. He told them the produce man asked for some. General said "well it's a little early they might be a few. ""I guess I could run over to Corner and see some of them Bagwell boys." "They might have some early greens." Shorty told him to go ahead.

The next morning General headed over to Corner. It was about 18 miles away. He first went over by Hoyt's. There were three of the boys, Hoyt, Glenn, and John. He went to Hoyt's and he told him there's was just not high enough. So General went on over to Glenn's. Told him what he was looking for. That there was a produce man in St Louis looking for greens. Glenn said "I doubt if mine is big enough, but I got some planted down in the bottoms on the creek." "I haven't looked at them in two or three days let's run down there and look at them." They got down there and they were about 5 inches high. Glenn said "I sure would like to cut that order but there not quite ready." "When would you need them?" General said "well by next Wednesday." "That will be five days from now." Glenn said "well General they'll grow plenty." "They will grow five inches by then." "Just count on a hundred bushel." General said "Can you stand 1.50 a bushel for the greens with no ice?" Glenn said "yeah that will be a good deal for me to just cut them and dip them and not have to ice them." So they made the deal and General said he would send a truck to pick up the greens.

CHAPTER TWENTY-SEVEN
Big Jim

Ed Miller Blount County sheriff had men out four days looking for that missing agent. He hadn't found out anything. He called Big Jim and told him Jim we've had four men out looking and we can't find anything. We can't even locate the car. Big Jim said "well let me get back in touch with Edgar and see what he says." Ed said "well ok let me know if there is anything else we need to do." "We will do all we can." So Big Jim got Washington office on the phone and told the lady he needed to talk to Mr. Hoover. The lady asked "may I ask who's calling ?" and he said "yes maam this is Big Jim Folsom the governuh of Alabama."

Mr. Hoover came to the phone Big Jim told him they hadn't found anything. He said "Edgar I still think everything's going to be alright." "The sheriff is still looking around and hasn't found out anything." "Them's good old boys up there." "They may be making a little bit of dranking whiskey but I still think everything is going to be alright." Edgar told Jim, "Jim we have waited long enough." "I have been in touch daily with the Birmingham office and they are going to pull agents out of Atlanta." "We are coming in with at least 50 agents." "You need to have some men ready and get the sheriff on standby." "We are going to find out what happened to my man."

In the meantime, Cracker's look out's. His little mafia, was talking to the sheriff deputies that something big was going on so Cracker let it leak out that there might be something going on down at Bangor Cave. He did so maybe he could keep everybody off the big deal. Big Jim called Ed Miller and told him "to get ready, in a few days Edgar Hoover is going to wrap that place up" "I will be providing state men and you have your county boys ready. ""I hate this but this is the way it is." It had already got to Ed Miller that there might be something going on down around Bangor Cave. He knew that Cracker Black knew that area real well so he got Cracker lined up to help him check it out. He told Cracker that "Hoover was gearing up to bring 50 agents in and Big Jim is bringing state men." "I am bringing in my men. I know you know this area real well." "You do a lot of hunting and everything so I want you to help me coordinate this thing. "Cracker said "Well yeah Ed I'll help anyway I can, but you know I ain't going in them woods." Said "them dam moonshiners will kill you." "I'll help anyway I can but I ain't going in them woods." Ed said "well me and you will get together tomorrow and figure it out."

So they met the next morning but, Cracker told him again that he wasn't going in the woods. He said "I'll help anyway I can but when you hem them dam moonshiners up they'll kill you." "I ain't ready to go right yet." Ed said "well tell me your plan." Cracker said "well I worked on it last night bring half of the federal agents to meet at Garden City on the railroad and half of them at Bangor." "Let them come north on the railroad and these come south on the railroad." "You know Bangor is on the eastside of the railroad." "Bring your county and state men off the Blountsville road and the little road that runs from Bangor to the Blountsville road and you'll have that thing covered up." Said "if there's anything down there and they run you'll have them in a triangle so you ought to be able to catch them." Ed said "that sounds like a good idea." So

Cracker said "if there is any other way I can help you let me know." "But I think you can handle it." "I got it lined up and I ain't going in them woods." Ed said "yeah I don't blame ye you got a family to think about."

CHAPTER TWENTY-EIGHT
Nobody Gets Caught

In the meantime, Cracker got a hold of Shorty and told him what was coming down. It was coming off on a Wednesday. He told Shorty that he had thought about it and said we got our whiskey hid pretty good down there between the river and Garden City. The whiskey they had in the woods was hid pretty good. Cracker went on to say, "I am going to have Big George not to have anybody in the woods on Wednesday except the lookout man to see if anything happens on that side." "We ain't going to ship no whiskey on Wednesday said we don't want nobody get caught." "Main thing is that nobody gets caught." If they find the Bangor still or the other one we don't want anybody to get caught." Shorty said "No you don't want anybody get caught."" I already got the produce lined up and General got the turnip greens lined up." Cracker said "that's fine I was figuring on shipping the produce right on." "I done thought of that." "If we don't ship on the day the agents come in that's going to look pretty funny." Cracker told Shorty to go on and have everything lined up "we want everything to go on just like it's been going." "We may have to ship produce only the next week." "We don't know."

Cracker went over and caught up with Red Turner and told him that the whiskey was already in the woods. That everything was all set-up for you another trip to Memphis. Cracker said "Red I don't want to get into the details but there's something big about to happen the last of the week." "I want you to haul this load the niggers will be down on the river and will have the whiskey on the side of the road at the set time." "Leave the Buick and come on back in your car." "Collect for the load and come back." "Don't come see me just go ahead and get your money out and I will check up with you later." Cracker went on to see Big George. He said "I don't want anybody in the woods." "We are going to shut the whole thing down." "The only guy will be the watchman." "He will be far enough away he can get away." "Make sure you tell the others to stay at home." "The only other thing I want is the fastest two niggers in the bunch;" Big George wanted to know why. Cracker said "well this Bangor cave deal has to look like it is more than a one man operation." "The way they going to come in there is an opening on top of the cave by the river." "They want be anybody up there." "The only thing I want them to do is be seen by the agents and then head for the river." "There won't be anybody lined up down there so they can get away." "We will put them a little boat on the river so they can get away." So Cracker left. He had been gone a few minutes and George picked out the two that he wanted to run. So he got them headed that away. Little Willie went to dancing around and poppin his butt singing "Ain't going back to no cotton patch, I ain't going back to no cotton patch, I ain't seed no cotton patch, what cotton patch?" Big George grabbed Little Willie and pulled him to one side. "Willie you better calm down cause if they catch us you gonna wish you could seed a cotton patch."

CHAPTER TWENTY-NINE
Better Run Fast

The two that were going to run were named Zeb and Raymond. Big George and Little Willie on Tuesday night after shutting everything down and made sure everybody was gone home, Zeb and Raymond went down to the river and got a boat to put in the river so they could paddle up the river about a quarter of a mile up the mulberry river. They actually carried two boats up the river. Big George told them they would make big money for doing this. More money then they ever saw. It was about two miles to the cave and Big George carried up there and stationed them out." I want you Zeb and your buddy to spend the night." "The agents will be coming in here in the morning early." "The sheriffs will be coming in from the Blountsville Road before daylight." "Ya'll be watching for them." "When they come in from the railroad I want you to get out in the open and make a bunch of noise so they see you and then take off running and get out of here." They said "yes Suh Mr. George ain't nobody gonna catch us." Big George and Little Willie went back and got their boat and went back down the river. Zeb and Raymond got in place and ready for the night.

Now on Tuesday morning Ed Miller the sheriff had met with the head FBI men and got together on the plan. Ed Miller asked them how they planned on transporting all of your agents up there. The head guy asked "well what you suggest." Ed said "well bring them on a greyhound bus." "That way there won't be a lot of vehicles coming in." "People are used to seeing the bus come and go." "Come in up there at Bangor where the road crosses the railroad." "I'll have you one county man there that knows the area real well." "He'll lead half the agents up the track." "I'll have another county man to get the ones that get off in Garden City and lead them down the track." "We will need to this right before daylight." "That way we can sneak up on anybody out there." The next morning the county men met the bus and got the agents in at Bangor and the other half there at Garden City above the Mulberry River. They had all the state men on the Blountsville road. The county men were on the cut-off from the Blountsville Road. They had a set time at 6:30 am right at daylight to move in on the cave area.

CHAPTER THIRTY

A Clean Getaway

Now old Ely lived there in the cave. They kept him plenty of groceries in the cave. It was just like having air conditioning in the cave so he didn't even bother going home. Now Zeb and Raymond could see the revenuers lining up on the railroad. When they started coming off the railroad toward the cave. Zeb and Raymond lay low until they got about 72 yards from them and then they walked out like they were walking through the woods. Then they looked up and acted like they saw them and turned toward the river and hauled ass as fast as they could go. All the federal, state, and county moved on in for the kill. The feds got to the cave before anybody. Then the state and county showed up. Up until then they hadn't caught anybody except old Ely. They found two vats of whiskey that was in the process and about 150 gallon of whiskey in jugs. They felt like they had really done something. The head FBI man said we got to get this man talking. He ain't running this by himself. So Ed Miller got in there and started talking to Ely but, he wasn't talking and didn't even act like he could even hear them. About three or four agents had to make a report on how it came down one that came off the railroad said he saw five niggers and a white man running through the woods, and another one said he saw the five niggers but didn't see a white man.

In the meantime Zeb and Raymond had gotten to the river and got in their boat. There was one agent that had stayed up on the trestle on the railroad bridge. He saw them coming down the river in the boat. He used his radio to tell his boss there were two niggers coming down the river in a boat what did he want him to do? His boss said you have to stop them. Zeb and them came on down. The agent was hollering move over to the bank and stop. They kept paddling down the river. The agent took a few pop shots at them. The bullets hit the water all around them. Raymond said "Zeb I'll hold my hands up like we are giving up and you paddle us over to the bank." So Raymond held his hands up. They were about 50 yards below the bridge at that time. The agent was up on the railroad trestle. It would take him a while to get over there. So they paddled over to the bank Raymond still had his hands up. Zeb got out of the boat and tied it up. They eased out of the boat under some trees and when they got their chance hauled ass up the bank and away from there. They made a clean getaway.

Back at the cave they were still trying to get Ely to talk. He wouldn't talk. They had a big time dumping the vats and dumping all the mesh out. They poured the whiskey out. The head FBI man asked Ed Miller what they ought to do. Somehow or other we have to get this guy to talk. It's a much bigger operation then just one or two guys. Ed said you go ahead make your reports to Birmingham and let them do what they have to do. I am going to let the state men report to the governor. I'll go ahead and take him up here and put him in jail at Garden City. Maybe a night or two in jail will make him start talking.

This was Wednesday morning and all the farmers got their crews in the fields picking their produce and getting ready to haul it to Garden City. About 10:00 General sent a truck to Corner for the greens. He told the driver to come back through Warrior and get a 1000 pounds of snow ice to ice the greens. General also sent a truck to Hog Mountain to pick up the tomatoes. All the farmers got the produce gathered and on the trucks. They started rolling in over at Garden City. The turnip green truck came in and the tomato truck. Shorty came on in with the big truck and decided to hang around there in stead of going back home. General said "Short you got a bigger load then you been having. Aren't you going to be heavy?" Short said "well yeah now Dan don't have as many watermelons as he has been having." "You know Marty really wanted those greens so I am going to take a chance."

They got all the produce loaded and it was just about dark. Shorty was able to pull out a little earlier then usual for St Louis. About one o'clock in the morning he got to the scales over there about Tupelo. He started easing up getting his front axle on the scales. One of the scale men came easing up beside him acting like he was guiding him on to the scales. When he got the chance he said "Shorty the big man out of Jackson is here." "Don't worry about any whiskey." Shorty said "well don't worry I don't have none." The scale man said "you know if you are over I am going to have to charge you." Shorty said "well, said that's fine." They weighed the front axle and he was fine. He pulled on up and got his pull wheels. He was barely over. He pulled on up and weighed the trailer and he was 1500 pounds over on the trailer axle. The state man walked up and said "Driver pull off to one side and bring in your registration and driver's license." Shorty said "Yes sir." He pulled on off the scales and got all his paperwork out and walked into the scale house and laid them on the desk. The state man said "Mr. Thomas are you in the habit of coming through our state and breaking our laws of being overweight." Shorty said "well, we don't have a scale down there to check our weight and sometimes it just happens." The state man said "Mr. Thomas this is going to cost you 28.00 cash before you can leave with this load of produce." He asked him what all he had on there. Shorty said turnip greens, cantaloupes, peaches, watermelons and tomato.

The state man said "I ought to make you unload some of it to make it legal but, since its produce I am going to let you carry it on." Shorty said, "Well, I appreciate that." One of the scale men wrote up the over weight ticket and Shorty paid it. Shorty had spent several hours at the scales. That made him run late that morning. He was following the old truck route through Tupelo. It was getting just about daylight when this boy about seven years old with real black hair wearing a pair of overalls ran out into his yard. He ran down by the road and began to pump his arm up and down wanting Shorty to blow the air horn. Shorty gave him 3 or 4 longs honks. Just as Shorty was passing by the mailbox he read the name Vernon Presley written on it.

CHAPTER THIRTY-ONE

They Got Their Man
or So They Thought

After everybody got everything wound up over at the cave, everybody left to go make their reports. Ed Miller carried Ely up there and locked him up in the Garden City jail. He told them what he was going to do. Let him stay in jail a day or two to see if he would talk. All the state men made their reports and got them in to Montgomery. The federal men got their reports into the Birmingham office. The Birmingham office then sent the reports into Washington. Mr. Hoover was satisfied that they had busted up an illegal whiskey operation but, he wasn't satisfied that they had not found his agent. He called Big Jim and told him that while he was satisfied about the bust up of an illegal operation he wasn't happy that they had not found his man. He told Jim that he was going to keep 12 agents in the area until they found out what happened to his agent. In turn Big Jim called Ed Miller and told him what was going on and that Hoover wanted him to put about 4 of his men with the agents asking questions and what not trying to find out what happened to his man. So Ed Miller got his chief that he wanted him to pick out 4 of his best men to work with the agents starting the next week and keep on till they find out what happened. Word filtered down through the deputies till it reached Cracker's henchmen. That there would be agents in the area until they find out what happened to the agent. So Cracker got in touch with Big George and anybody else Red Turner and whoever needed to know. He told Big George to tell all his people to lay low and stay out of the woods that everything was called off for the time being.

On Thursday that afternoon, Ed Miller came by the jail and started trying to question Old Ely Merrell. Ely acted like he didn't even know what he was saying. Ed Miller told the police that he was going to let him stay in there till Monday and let him soak. I think he'll be ready to talk about Monday. Ya'll feed him and everything Blount County will pick up the tab. I'll be back around on Monday.

Shorty got back in Sunday. Cracker went by to see him and told him what was going on. He said as long as Marty wants produce we'll go ahead and load produce. He told them to go ahead and coordinate it with the farmers as usual. "We'll haul produce but there want be any whiskey involved for a while." Big George will have a crew up there to load the produce as usual and I'll be around so everything will look as normal as possible.

There was this family of Reno's that lived down below Bangor. They was about five or six of them. They were a mean bunch that hated niggers. There was another family that ran with them the Mackenzie's. They had heard what was going on. A couple of them went up to Garden City to see if they could find out what was going on. They were talking to one of the policemen there. They were asking about what was going on.

One of the policemen there told them everything they knew. "We got the only nigger they caught in jail. He won't talk though. "The head Reno said "we'll make him talk." "We can make any nigger talk." The cop said "we can't let you go in there and make him talk." "Me and my buddy have been working on this case and would like to get credit for helping solve it." "You think you can make him talk? "Reno said "I guarantee we can make him talk." The cop said "ok I'll tell you what I'm going to do." "Early tonight just after dark me and my buddy will be on the north side of town patrolling around." "Ya'll come in here and you'll find a key in the right hand top desk drawer." "Unlock him and take him out." Reno said "yea we'll take him down at the baptizing hole at the river." "We'll make him talk." So that night the Reno's and three of the Mackenzie boys were with them. There was five or six of the Reno boys. They came in and unlocked the cell and took Ely out and loaded him in the car. Big George and Little Willie just happened to be coming by the jail and saw what was going on. They could tell it wasn't right. They headed down to Cracker's and told him what was going on. They told Cracker they was headed down to the baptizing hole down at the river and Cracker asked "Big George do you know George Hardin." Big George said "Yes Suh I know right where George lives." Cracker said "you go there and tell him to get some of his buddies and meet me at the baptizing hole just as fast as he can." So by the time Cracker got down to the baptizing hole some of the Reno's were already there and had a big fire built. They had Ely tied to the tree and had a big limb they had hit him with a few times. Said "nigger you better talk." They would hit him again and say nigger you better talk. Cracker stepped in and tried to stop them, but there was too many of them. They threatened to whoop him and tie him up. He did delay it enough scuffling with them and threatening them. Finally they tied Cracker up threatening to hurt him. They hit Ely a couple more times saying talk nigger. About that time two cars of Ku Klux drove up. They got out had their hoods and robes on. They got out and did not say anything. The lead Reno boy said "now you'll talk nigger." The head Ku Klux walked up and cut Ely loose and cut Cracker loose. By then the white pastor and the black pastor had heard what was happening. They got down there. The Reno boy wanted to know what's going on. He thought the KKK should be helping them. Reno still saying, "We going to make that nigger talk." The head Ku Klux turned around and looked him straight in the eye and said "Ely can't talk." Reno said "well why didn't he tell us he couldn't talk?" That Ku Klux backed handed Reno and knocked him for a flip. And the other Ku Klux, four to a car eight in all, had them some hickory sticks and they whooped up on the Reno's pretty good and ran them off. The Ku Klux turned Ely over to the preachers and said take care of him and make sure somebody stays with him.

CHAPTER THIRTY-TWO
Trot Line Fishin

The word didn't get back to Ed Miller and everything until Monday morning when he came over to question Ely. He found out what happened and found out the Ely couldn't talk. He got with the Garden City Police and chewed them out about what happened. They said Ah we wasn't there and didn't know what happened. He threatened to have them charged. He went over and talked to the two preachers to take care of Ely. I ain't going to lock him up. He can't talk so I'll put yall in charge of him to take care of.

That evening the federal agents that were going to stay in the area come up and got with the sheriff. He had four of his deputies was to work with the agents everyday. Ed Miller got with them and said there was no need for him to run in everyday and have to know what was going on for them to get together every morning and plan in what direction pair off in four groups and decided what sections they was going to work. They started going around in three counties a big part of three counties. Looking around in the woods and asking people questions anything they could find out.

Shorty went ahead and lined up a load of produce for Wednesday and farmers brought in their produce about the same thing they had been bringing. Big George had his crew over there so things would look normal. Cracker was hanging around. He had a little hand in the produce deal. They got it loaded and he headed out.

About after three days of the agents looking around and asking questions, walking the woods and what have you, Ed Miller got with them and having a brain session. He said I can kindly understand us not finding the man but, what I don't understand is us not finding the car. So they talked over everything they were planning to do the next day or two in order to try to find the car and the man. Cracker was easing around telling his group to just cool it. Go fishing and work in the field and do whatever they wanted to do. As long as there were agents in the field they were not going to do anything with the whiskey.

Now on Friday night Warren Hogeland that lived over about Locust Fork him and four of his boys that ranged in age about 6 to 17 were putting out trot lines down on the Warrior River down close to Trafford. On Friday evenings they always put out trot lines and camp out. They were camping that night. The next morning they were running their trot lines, they had run the lower three lines. They took off about four or five catfish, one weighed about 10 pounds a big yellow cat. They came on up to the upper lines and started running it. One of the boys, there was three of them in the boat, said we got one. They got on out there and it was about a five pound blue cat. They started easy on out across there and the water was a little bit swift there really deep and swift. Warren said "boys I believe we got a big one." "This thing is tight I believe we got a big one." He kept pulling on the line and pulling on the line and looked around. He said "No I don't believe it's a fish." A big one probably got on and went down and got under a rock. He kept working with it and working with it and finally come loose. When it did it came up and had a car mirror in the line. Warren just laid the mirror down in the boat and went on and ran the line all the way across. They didn't catch anything. They was going to bait the line back out that afternoon. They went back over to their camp and he got to thinking he told one of his boys to run back down there and bring him that mirror. He went down and brought it back to his daddy. Warren said "man that mirror hadn't been in this water too long." Said "it ain't been in there a long time at all." Warren said "let's go back out there." The oldest boy said "Daddy I'll dive down in there if you'll pull the trot line up where I won't get hung I'll dive down in there and see if there anything down there. "So he was a good diver and swimmer so he dived down. The water was muddy so he couldn't see that much. He dove down and came back up in about thirty seconds and said "daddy there's a car down there." So they pulled him back into the boat and went back over to the fire. Warren didn't think that much about it to start with. They were going on with their fishing and everything. They baited the lines back out that night. He remembered he had heard something about the FBI had an agent missing. He also heard about the whiskey still blow-up in Bangor cave. He still didn't put it all together right away. They went on with their fishing the rest of the weekend. On Sunday he got to thinking about it a little heavier and decided he better get word to Ed Miller and tell him what happened. So Monday Warren got up and went to Oneonta and got a hold of Ed Miller that him and his boys were putting out trot lines and told him what happened that his boy dove down in there and found a car down on the bottom of the rocks. When Ed Miller heard that a flag went straight up. He figured they might have something. He got a hold of the state and federal. He said we need to get that car out. The mirror wasn't enough to go on by itself. So they started making plans to pull the car out. They decided getting everything ready that they'd pull it out on Wednesday morning.

CHAPTER THIRTY-THREE
He Better Not Be in There

In the meantime ,they had a bunch of State, Federal, and County. The word had got around thought two or three counties so on Wednesday morning they had a big group out there. News people from Birmingham, Nashville, Montgomery. Ed Miller lined up Johnny Calvert from out there at county line, he was the only one that had heavy equipment, and he had a bulldozer. He was a coal miner. The coal mines were all under ground where they used mule and wagons but, he had a bull dozer to face up the mine where they start digging the coal. They got him over there on Wednesday morning and like I said they was five or six hundred people, news people and even had one old guy selling hotdogs. During the time the sheriff was getting everything lined up, the federal and state and a couple of county guys still didn't have any ideals what they were looking for. They were still investigating how the car got in the river. They went up on the bluff where the road runs right beside the river up on the high bluff and found where all the limbs were broke out. Kindly in a trail go down the side of the bluff. They got down there on the bottom and found where the top had been broke out of a big pine tree. They decided that the car would have probably landed on the bank but it got in the top of the big pine tree and it pitched it on out into the water.

They got the bull dozer in place on the south side of the river. Ed Miller had Warren over there to show them where the car was at. The river was real muddy so you couldn't see down in the river. They had five or six professional divers there to help them out. The bull dozer had a little wench on it so they started pulling out the cable. They had about eight men that were pulling it out by hand until they got about waist deep. Then they pulled it on out there with a boat. They had about four or five little motor boats with a 3 and half motors on them Johnson and Mercury's. The rest of them were paddle boats. They hooked the cable to one of them boats. It couldn't pull it by itself. It was too hard pull off that reel. They got two more boats in front and tied ropes to them. All three of those boats barely could pull the cable out. But they finally got out there.

Warren had done showed the sheriff where the car was at. We are approximately over it right now. They had a couple of divers go down but it was so muddy even with diving goggles on it was too muddy to see. They were afraid to let them get in the car because they were afraid they would get caught and drown. They didn't have any breathing equipment.

Three divers went back in with the cable. The car was upside down. When it went into the water it landed on its top. The divers didn't have any problem hooking a cable to it. They started slowly moving the car out of the water. They were all wondering if the agent was still in the car. Warren said "well if he's still in the car in this water the yellow cats have already eat him up." One agent spoke up and said "yeah you may be right but there would still be some bones left."

They were slowly pulling it on in. It was still under the water. The newsman and some sheriff deputies were making them back up. They were right on the bank with their cameras. They had to make the crowd back up. There was a crowd up on the bluff and down below there on the bridge watching. Of course Cracker was over there trying to help them anyway he could. Trying to solve any problems. In the meantime, Big George and Little Willie were parked up on the bluff a watching. There were quite a few people up there with them watching. They were betting as to whether or not the man was still in the car or not. Little Willie whispered to Big George and said "he ain't in there, that man ain't in there." George told him to shut up. In a minute Little Willie said "He better not be in there."

CHAPTER THIRTY-FOUR
Fine Tooth Comb

Cracker was standing on the south bank with the other crowd and was thinking that finding the car was the best thing to happen to him and for the whiskey operation. They finally got the car in shallow enough water where they could see part of it. They eased it on out and one of the agent who knew the car and worked with the missing agent said yeah that's looks like the car but we'll know when we run the tag number. They got it pulled on out and first checked to see if he was in there. They couldn't find any sign of the agent so they checked the tag and sure enough that was the car they were looking for. So they had a little brain session. They were pretty sure that the man was dead. They didn't know if he had died in the river or maybe had managed to make it to the bank of the river and died there. So they were going to put on a big search of the banks.

They got a wrecker and hooked to the car and pull it in to FBI headquarters in Birmingham. They wanted to go over it with a fine tooth comb and see if they could find something that would help with the investigation. The Sheriff, head FBI man and the head State man got together and organized a search of what boats were there. They had a lot of volunteers and let them all get started that day. But they didn't find anything. The FBI man said "we will get together in the morning, get all the boats available and volunteers and let's get in here and try to find this agent." "We'll put thirty or forty agents in boats up and down the river." "They will have their walkie talkie's and if anybody finds anything they can get word back to headquarters." That day they ended their search at dark. Nobody found anything. They all had the word to come back about seven o'clock the next morning to launch the big search. One old farmer standing over there said "that man may be in Mobile by now."

Cracker left out from down there a few minutes before dark and got in his pick-up and got in it and went across the bridge headed back to Garden City. When he got to the top of the bluff he saw Big George and Little Willie standing there watching. He slowed down and motioned for them to come on. They went about five miles and pulled over. Cracker stopped first with Big George stopping in behind him. They stopped for a minute. Cracker just told them to play it cool, just play it cool.

Before all the law men left the river that night the state, county and FBI got together and made their plans on how the search was going to go. The head FBI man told them that Mr. Hoover said anything they need that he would get it to us to help find the agents. "All the volunteers that have boats we will let them work the river." "They will have agents with them along with a few Federal boats." "I want the State to get his volunteers and take one side of the river and the Sheriff to take his volunteers and search the other side of the river." "They are getting two trucks out of Atlanta that have stoves and blankets." He wanted all the volunteers to bring them something to eat during the day but, where they ended the search that night they would have these trucks set up to cook supper. They would have blankets to rest on and be able to cook a good breakfast the next morning before they started out. Next morning they got everybody organized. The State was on one side of the river and the County was on the other side. In all they had about thirty-five boats with two men to the boat. The County had about thirty-five men on his side. The State had about twenty-five or thirty. The FBI head said to look under every rock and in every hole. They were also going to look the river bottom all the way down. This thing could last about three days.

CHAPTER THIRTY-FIVE
The Search

The load of produce that went out on that Wednesday had a few peaches, cantaloupes, watermelons and greens. But when Shorty got to St Louis he told Marty that would all the peaches, cantaloupes and watermelons. Marty asked him about tomatoes? Shorty said "yeah there's going to be tomatoes until frost on that mountain." Marty said "well while I'm making a little money, you're making a little money and the farmers are making a little money let's just haul tomatoes and greens." "After the tomatoes are gone and everybody is satisfied we'll just haul greens for a little while." Shorty said "ok and made it on back home." He told Cracker what the plan was on the produce. Cracker said "that's fine you and General just keep it going." "When everything quiets back down we might try to put a little whiskey on but we ain't cranking back up just yet." "It will be a while before we get all the way cranked back up."

The search got started that morning and people on each bank were looking hard under everything under every log and rock. The people in the river were checking out every hole and poking sticks in every hole and under every rock see if they could get a hold of anything. By lunch time they had made it about a mile and half down the river. They stopped and had a good lunch and rested a little bit then they headed on down the river. The Sheriff and the head FBI man got together and figured about how far they were going to get by that afternoon so they sent a vehicle out to bring their trucks in as close to the river as they could get. This would be about where they would get to by that afternoon. They began the search that afternoon and everybody was working hard and made a little over another a mile and half that afternoon. They got down close to where the truck was so they called the search off for the night. People were cooking and handing out blankets. They told the workers to go put their blankets where they wanted to sleep and then come back. They had some army trays they handed the food out on. The people began to pair off and build fires and settle in. It looked like the army was camped out.

All the men got lined up and got them a good meal took about an hour to feed them all. They got bowl of beef stew and a big chunk of corn bread. They had either cold milk or coffee to drink. They all got fed and got a good night's rest and the cook crew started waking everybody up the next morning. They had scrambled eggs, sausage, grits, and coffee for breakfast. A little bit after daylight they had everybody fed. The crews began to get with their leaders and get ready to go back out. The cook crew had to get everything cleaned up. They had to get the truck loaded and headed on down to where they would be about lunch time.

They made it about 2 mile of terrain on each side of the river it wasn't quite as rough as it had been in the river. They made it to where the lunch trucks were. They stop about an hour ate lunch and rested a little bit. They headed on down the river like it had been being. The cook truck had to get ready and go. Everybody else headed on to the search down the river.

About three thirty that afternoon the FBI headquarters in Birmingham called the head FBI in charge of the search and told him to call off the search. They didn't tell him why just to call it off. So he got busy and got word to everybody up and down the river. The agents had walkie talkies. He told them all to come in.

They got the search called off and everybody headed toward home. They were all asking questions but, they didn't have any answers for them right then. In the meantime one of the head FBI men was on his way to meet with the sheriff, FBI agents and the state men. He got out there about five o'clock that afternoon. The FBI, sheriff, and the state men wanted to know why they had called the search off. The man told them that the man was not in the river and never did go in the river. They wanted to know how did he know he said well the switch on the car was turned off and said if he had of went off the bluff on accident he would not have turned the switch off. The motor wasn't running when he went into the water. They took the motor apart and there was no water on top of the pistons so they felt sure the agent did not go in the river.

By the next afternoon most everybody that was involved in the search had found out why they called the search off. Cracker had also found out why they called the search off. Of course Cracker was already looking forward and making plans. They knew they would not find a body, but they didn't know it would end up like this. That the FBI believed never really went into the river. So since they didn't believe he ever went into the river they would have to be real cautious.

One evening a few days later, Delton Franklin came in from the mines. It was a little after daylight. He farmed a little. So normally he would work a little bit and then go to bed and rest. He would get up later that afternoon to get ready to go back to the mines. This particular afternoon when he got up he heard a lot of noise down at the barn. Now Mrs. Franklin worked at the Post Office in town so she didn't get back in until late. He heard this noise so he went out and found kids hollering and laughing and the hogs were all cutting up. Those boys had found the whiskey that was in the barn. Delton had been carrying some to his friends at the mines to have when they got off every morning. The boys had poured it in the hog trough and got the hogs drunk. They probably got a little drink themselves because they were all raising cane and cutting up. The hogs were jumping and squealing and having a big time. Delton got them down out of the loft and said "Boys", his two little toe headed boys, Allen and Mack. He said "Boys I ought to tear yall up. But, if yall want tell you mama what happened I won't ." "But, if you tell mama I am going to tie you up in a tow sack and throw you in the river. "That seemed a pretty good reason to them to not tell mama. So as far as we know today Mama still doesn't know.

CHAPTER THIRTY-SIX
Keep On Haulin

That same night Cracker went over to catch up with Big George and tell him what was going on. "We are going to keep laying low." "I know that some of the boys may be needing some money, I know their working in the fields but they still may need some money." So he gave Big George enough to give them about 10 dollars a week. That was about half of what they could make in the field. So Big George said he would handle it.

Cracker went over to see Shorty and catch him up on what was happening. Now Shorty knew about the search and everything but he didn't know what had happened to the agent. He told him to just keep on hauling produce and whatever you got to haul Maters or Greens whatever it is. Big George will have a crew over there to load the produce whatever you got to haul. We just want to keep everything looking the same.

Now Mr. Hoover called the head man in Birmingham and they talked. Mr. Hoover said "well every investigation has been very visible. Maybe it's time to have a more covert investigation." So they decided to not include Mr. Big Jim Folsom in the next plans. They would also leave out the sheriff. They would handle it themselves. They would put about 12 agents in each area. "We don't care how long it takes." "We will get them a job and let them move in there." "Some of them can work at the sawmill, and the railroad in Hayden and Bangor." "They can move into the community and live in the community." The man said "yea when everybody is involved there are too many mouths involved so everybody knows everything."

Now Cracker knew they would have to be careful with everything. All he knew about J Edgar Hoover he knew he wouldn't just drop this thing so they had to be careful. That coming Wednesday Shorty left out with just tomatoes and greens. He got up there and told Marty that this would be the end of the tomatoes. Marty said that well if it's ok with you we'll just haul greens. Cracker had about one load of whiskey hid in the woods for St Louis and one load to Memphis. He wanted to get it out because he needed the money. He owed Mr. Sam for two loads of sugar and he owed for corn and other items he wanted to get these paid for. He wasn't really hurting for money but, he didn't want to have to pay for all this out of his own pocket.

Shorty got on back in off of that trip from delivering the tomatoes and greens. So he went to see General and told him Marty said to just keep hauling turnip greens and said he could haul about 300 bushels. General said "well we will cut turnip greens." "Our's is big enough now and I found out that Coy and Brady," now Brady was Shorty and General's youngest brother, "have a patch." He said he would line it up and they could cut a 100 bushel and he would cut a hundred bushel. He could also get a hundred bushel from Corner. So if Shorty didn't call it off they would have the load ready for next Wednesday. Shorty said that would be fine.

Saturday morning Cracker went in there at Mr. Sam's store to pick up a few items, of course Big Ben and Little Ben were in there running around. You hardly saw Mr. Sam in the daytime that you didn't see Little Ben. Cracker told him he was working on a deal to get him the rest of his money for the stuff he owed him for. Mr. Sam said well just take your time and get it when you can. It's not a big deal. Mr. Sam said "Cracker you going to go hear old Hank sang." Cracker said, "Hank?" Mr. Sam said "yeah Hank Williams." "He's coming to town in two weeks and put on a show at the school house." "I think me and Little Ben will go" Cracker said, "I don't know, I'd like to go." "If I can I'm going to go." Cracker left and started doing some strong thinking that this would be a good time to get the rest of the whiskey out of town. Because everybody would be at the Hank Williams show. Cracker started making his plans.

CHAPTER THIRTY-SEVEN
The Hank Williams Show

Hank Williams Momma was running the show. She was handling his money and making all the engagements. Along about 1945-46 Hank was performing in the Louisiana Hayride every Saturday night. In between Saturday's he would go other places and put on a show. So when Mrs. Williams came up there to talk to some of the business leaders in Garden City about Hank coming up there and putting on a show. They were getting everything lined up and she said yeah. So they set it, see it's getting on into October, and they set it for a Thursday night the third week in November. They got everything set-up except Mrs. Williams asked them were the colored people going to be able to come. They said no, now when they have revival we go hear the preaching and they come to our revivals but things like this we just don't mix. She said "well we will just call the whole thing off then" said "we have a lot of colored friends down there in South Alabama where we are from and we got one colored boy playing in the band his name is Charlie Pride." "We need this engagement and the money but we won't do it if we can't make sure there's a house full and the colored people can come." So the business men put there heads together and decided that would be the thing to do. So it was set for a Thursday night the third week in November.

When Cracker found out when the Hank Williams show was going to be, he started making preparations to get those other two loads of whiskey hauled. The next Wednesday all the farmers brought their greens in to load. General sent a truck over to Bagwell's to get theirs and Brady and Coy brought their greens. The black folks were there to ice and load the greens. In the meantime, Cracker got with Shorty that the next load would have greens and whiskey to haul, Shorty said well we will work it out. Cracker told him it would have to be done on Thursday night he told him it was because of the big Hank Williams show. Everybody would be occupied with that so it would be safe to load. So Cracker went on and got with Red. Red said yeah I'm about to run out of money and need to make some. Cracker said "well I believe we will be able to open back up one day but right now we can't." "I need to move this whiskey I got on hand." Red said "yeah I'll be ready but the only thing is I left that Buick up there and got my Ford back." Cracker said "well you get in touch with Jesse and it will be the same deal." "I'll give him fifty dollars to run interference for you and if he gets caught I'll pay the fine." So Red lined it up with Jesse for the next Thursday night.

So Shorty knew they would hauling the rest of that whiskey the next coming Thursday night and he knew he wouldn't be able to haul quite as many greens. So he got in touch with General and told him Marty didn't want as many on this next trip. He wanted to cut it down to about 250 bushel. General smelled a rat. He didn't say anything right then but he said "Well Bagwell helped us get started with greens and besides that I am making a little money on them so I'll go ahead and let him cut a hundred bushel and I'll let Brady and Coy cut 75 bushel and I'll cut 75." Shorty said "yeah that'll be fine. It will probably be back to 300 bushel next time."

Now Red Turner went and hooked up with Jesse and told him the deal. It would be the same deal as before. He would make fifty dollars and Cracker would pay the fine if something happened.

Jesse said "yeah I'll do it, but what are you doing tomorrow?" and Red said "nothing why?" "I want to check out my getaway route." "I don't want what happened last time to happen again." So the next day Jesse and Red took a trip over there instead of going back toward Cordova and picked a route going toward Empire. He made sure there wasn't any bridges out and all. He told Red "I'm not going to drive my Chevrolet" said "I'm going to borrow daddy's Ford." "He don't drive it fast but that thing will run like a scaled ass ape." "That way the law won't know it was the same person as it was before." So they got everything lined up and waited on Thursday night to come.

Finally Thursday night rolled around and everything was going with the famers and everything was lined up for George to get the whiskey out of the woods and down the river for the loading site. Shorty had heard about Hank Williams show would be going on. He told Cracker that he would just come over and go to the show and when it was over he would come and get the truck and go. Cracker said "yeah that'll work."

Shorty was telling Mrs. Thomas about it and their little old boy named Bobby Joe. He heard about it and said "Daddy can I go to the Hank Williams show please can I go to the Hank Williams show." Shorty said "well son if your mama don't care me and you will go to the Hank Williams show and you can go with me to St Louis." Boy Bobby Joe was tickled to death. In the meantime, the word of the Hank Williams deal had got out far and near. So the Thomas boys heard about it and asked their daddy Mr. General if they could go. He said "well when we carry the greens over there we will just stay and go to the show." The Swan girls heard the Thomas' were going to get to go so they put in to go saying Daddy can we go they going to get to go, so Coy said "well ya'll might as well." So Mrs. Pauline decided she wanted to go. So Coy asked if they had everything lined up for the Hank Williams show.

CHAPTER THIRTY-EIGHT
Red and Jesse Make Their Plans

Red and Jesse had all their plans layed out. Jesse was going to be waiting at nine o'clock down at that off road just before you cross the big creek bridge before you get to Arkadelphia and follow him through when Red got there. Jesse decided he would go for part of the Hank Williams show. Jesse asked him his daddy if he could borrow his Ford pick-up. His daddy asked him why and Jesses said he was tired of driving that truck of his and just wanted to drive that Ford awhile. His momma said "where you going Jesse?" He said "I'm going to the Hank Williams show." She said "well I want to go to the Hank Williams show." Jesse said "well you and daddy can get in my pick-up and go." Said "I got some things I need to do after the show and I want have time to bring you home so you and daddy just go in my pick-up." Jesse sure didn't want momma on this trip.

All the business men in Garden City while they were planning the Hank Williams show wanted to make sure it was a big blow out. They wanted to be sure and have him back in another year. They decided to get word to all the community and all around. They said anybody that had spent at least three dollars in any store in town would get a free ticket. The ticket price was one dollar and so the word got out to everybody. They also decided that some people might not even have three dollars to spend in a store so all General Stores they came up with a deal where that if you brought them a chicken and dozen eggs, or a pound of butter then you could get a ticket to go to the show. Many people got to go that way but, there were quite a few that spent the three dollars.

It was getting on around 4:30 - 5:00; the show was to start about 7:30 pm. The farmers started coming in with their trucks. The Corner truck the one General sent to Corner to pick-up the greens came in. Then Coy and his drove came in and started unloading their greens. Lorene, the Swan girls mother, who was also a sister to Brady, Shorty and General, she decided to come to the show. She was in with them. They backed in to the dock and the Swann girls started unloading the greens so they made sure they had plenty of time to get to the show. Then General's bunch came in they had to bring an extra truck. Their son Harold the oldest boy drove the truck to haul all the other boys that came. General, Mrs. Pauline, and Paul was in the cab. Some of the boys were on the back with the turnip greens and the rest were in the truck with Harold. They all got in and got their greens unloaded. They got the greens unloaded and it was still early for the show so the whole group started visiting Mr. Sam's store and some of them had a little money to spend and some were just shopping.

CHAPTER THIRTY-NINE
Dan and Judd At It Again

Now Old Dan Ledbetter has heard all about the Hank Williams show. He knew who he was by listening to the radio. So he decided he would go to the show. Old Judd was his black buddy. Since the trial they had become buddies again. So he asked Judd to go to the show. Old Judd said "Mr. Dan I'd like to but you know there not going to let niggers in there." Mr. Dan said "Yeah there going to let niggers come to the show." "Mrs. Williams said they would not put on the show if they didn't let niggers in." So Judd asked Dan how much to get in. Mr. Dan said "it cost a dollar." Judd said "Mr. Dan I ain't got no dollar." Dan said "well I ain't got one neither." "You can bring a chicken they'll let you in for free if you bring a chicken." Judd said "Mr. Dan I ain't got no chicken." Dan said "I ain't got one neither but, Mrs. Jones down there right below me got too many chickens."

Old Dan ever since he heard you could bring a chicken and get in he has been getting a few ears of corn out of Deacon Brown's patch and shelling it and putting it out on the ground down there. Mrs. Jones had a chicken pen but some of them had been getting out because she had too many. Every evening the chickens had been showing up down at Dan's shack looking for that corn. So Dan and Judd around about 5 or 5:30 sprinkled some corn out there around the yard and them domin necker chickens were out there eating that corn so they snagged them one a piece. So when it came time to go to the show they showed up down there with a chicken under their right arm. They showed up to get in. It was almost time for the show start and people were lined up either they had their tickets that they had got at the store or was paying to get in. When it came Dan's time they didn't really notice the chicken. He had on a light colored jacket and the chicken was under it. So when he got up there they said "Now Dan that'll be a dollar "and Dan said, "I ain't got no dollar I got a chicken." That old domin Necker chicken had its head sticking out. They said "You can't get in for no chicken." Dan said "they been telling me for a week you could get in for a chicken or pound of butter and I got a chicken." Dan had not understood that he was supposed to go to the store and redeem it for a ticket. They said Dan "you and Judd get out of here with your chickens." Mr. General was right behind them so he stepped in to see what was happening. They told him that Dan and Judd were trying to get in with a live chicken and they cannot do that. Mr. General said "ya'll go outside and let your chickens loose and come back in and I'll pay your way in."

Shorty and Bobby Joe were running a little bit late but, they came in with the big rig and got it parked and had to rush before the show started. The police had two police cars and four policemen. They were busy directing traffic and showing people were to park. It was a big deal to them they had never seen traffic like this. There wound up being 350 white people and 50-60 black people. Along with Dan and Judd, they got them a seat.

Big George and his crew along with Little Willie come in and started icing the greens. They would not touch the liquid stuff until after the show started.

Chapter Forty
Let the Show Begin

Showtime finally got here boy that house was full packed about like sardines in a can. Everybody was all pumped up ready for the show. Hank's momma brought the band, their name was the "Drifting Cowboys", she brought them out to say a word or two before Hank came out. Mrs. Williams talked to the people a minute or two and told everyone how glad they were to be there and hoped everyone enjoyed the show. She introduced the band and said this is the Drifting Cowboys, on steel guitar you got Charlie Pride and the crowd just roared. Then Hank came through the curtain and she said now you have Hank Williams the King of Country. The crowd just roared and the top almost came off the school. Everybody was standing and cheering. He took his bows to a standing ovation. When the crowd settled down he said a few words and went to playing. (Song Starts) (Hear that lonesome whipper will he's sounds too blue to fly the midnight train is whining low, I'm so lonesome I could cry. I've never seen a night so long when time goes crawling by, the moon just went behind a cloud to hide its face and cry… music plays…. You ever seen a robin weep when leaves begin to die that means he lost the will to live I'm so lonesome I could cry… music plays….. The silence of a fallen star lights up a purple sky and as I wonder where you are I'm so lonesome I could cry.... Song ends) (Next song starts I tried so hard my dear to show that you're my every dream yet your afraid each thing I do is just some evil scheme, A memory from your lonesome past keeps us so far apart Why can't I free your doubtful mind and melt your cold cold heart. Another love before my time made your heart sad and blue so now my heart is paying now for things I didn't do. Anger and unkind words are said that make the teardrops start why can't I free you doubtful heart and melt your cold cold heart...) (Hey Hey good looking what you got cooking.. How's about cooking something up with me. Hey sweet baby don't you think maybe we can find us a brand new recipe.. I got hot rod ford and a two dollar bill, and I know a spot right over the hill, there's soda pop and the dancing free so if you want to have fun come along with me. Say hey good looking.....) (Listen to the rain a falling can't you hear that lonesome sound of my poor old heart is breaking because my sweet love ain't around...) (Oh plllleease don't let me love you just because I'm feeling blue oh plllleease don't let me kiss you cause I know you'll be untrue.. because your sweet dear I want to love you please stay away from my heart. Plllleease don't let me love you.....) (Oh why don't you love me like you use to do how come you treat me like a worn out shoe, my hairs still curly and my eyes are still blue.. Why don't you love me like you use to do....Ain't had no loving and kissin in along long while We don't get nearer or further than a country mile Why don't you spark me like you use to do and say sweet nothings like you use to do I'm the same old trouble that you been through so why don't you love me like you use to do.) Suddenly Hank threw his hands up and stopped the boy from playing right in the middle of that song and put his hand up to his ear and started listening...It was the Hummingbird running southbound about 80 miles an hour and he was listening to that. The train was coming through so fast you could feel the vibration in the school house. The train horn started sounding long and low Whonk whonk Whonk

Whonk Hank said boys let's sing em song about a train.. Music starts (I have a stories about trains but now I'll tell you about one that all the colored folks have seen she's a beauty of the south land listen to that whistle scream on the Pana American on her way to New Orleans. She leavin Cincinatta headed down that Dixie line when she passes that Nashville tower you can hear that whistle whine. Stick your head right out the window you can feel that southern breeze. You are on the Pana American on your way to New Orleans. Guitar plays....... If you're ever in the Southland and want to see the seen just get yourself a ticket on the Pana American Queen. There's Louisville, Nashville, Montgomery the cap of Alabama you pass right through them all when you are New Orleans bound. Leavin Cincinatta headed down that Dixie Line when she passes that Nashville tower you can hear that whistle whine. Stick your head right out the window you can feel that southern breeze. You're on the Pana American on your way to New Orleans.

CHAPTER FORTY-ONE

Momma Pearl Got Her Eye on the Situation

Now the show was going to last another hour but Jesse figured it was time he headed out so he could be down there sittin and waiting on Red. He got up and started out. Big Momma Taylor knowed something was up. She had kindly been keeping her eye on Jesse so when he started walking out Big Momma stood up but, Mr. Taylor took her by the arm and sat her back down. As Jesse went through the back door he spoke to Mr. Sam and Little Ben back there. Jesse got in his daddy's Ford to head out to meet Red. Little Willie and Big George and their crew done had the whiskey loaded and was already loading greens on top of it. They didn't have any trouble with the law tonight because they were real busy up at the school house.

Now Jesse got down there to his parking place waiting on Red. In about 20 minutes Red comes along. In a little bit Jesse passed him and went on over there on 78 hwy south of Jasper to the hide out for Red to pull in. Jesse stopped over there and got Red positioned and everything. Then Jesse went on into town. He knew 75% of the time the law would be sitting in front of City Hall on the main drag so he took some back streets. He went through town on the backstreets and got over there and headed back toward Birmingham on 78. He got over there where he could see the red light down there where the law was setting. Sure enough they were there. He timed the light where he would make it. He didn't want to run no red-light. Boy he floored that old Ford and when he went by the law he was probably already doing 60 70 mph and here they come. Red/Blue lights and sirens wide open. When Red saw them go by he pulled out and headed toward Memphis. The law was hanging pretty close to Jesse right on his tail until he cut through on some dirt roads. Of course they couldn't stay plum up with him then. Jesse got over to the Sipsy River on Low Water Bridge and a pretty sharp curve going into the bridge. He went on over the bridge and over a hill and hit a straight away there. He never did see their lights no more. He didn't know what happened but he though for sure something did.

By now the show was over and Big George and them got everything loaded and the tarp pulled over. Everything was ready for Shorty and Bobby Joe to pull out. They came down there to get ready to leave. General's bunch and Coy's bunch came down there to get their trucks and head for home.

The next day Jesse and his daddy with a couple of hired hands was pulling corn getting it ready to haul and come in for dinner. Pearl had dinner ready and they got washed up. Pearl asked Jesse "Jesse where did you go last night?" He said, "Well no where really." She said, "Now Jesse you tell me where you were." He said, "Now momma I don't have to tell you everywhere I go." "I'm grown now you know." And Pearl said "I heard on the radio that the Jasper Police run into the Sipsy River and almost drowned put they got out." Old Jesse said "Well wonder what happened." Pearl said "well they said on the radio they was chasing a black Ford pick-up truck with a Cullman county tag on it." Old Jesse said, "Well now that is something Momma." "But boy I'm sure glad they didn't get hurt."

CHAPTER FORTY-TWO
Puttin the Brakes On

There wasn't anymore whiskey to haul. It was all out of the woods. Cracker wasn't going to try to crank back up in the woods because there was still too many agents around. While Shorty was gone with this load of greens Clarence Mayfield out of Louisville got in touch with General, they usually shipped him cantaloupes and peaches. He told him they were needing greens up there if they could get them. Usually South Georgia would be kicking in by now. It was kind of like the turnip green capital, but they had a real dry summer and fall. It looked like it would be after Christmas before they would have any. General said let me check and I will get back with you. So General went over to Corner to see how theirs were looking. They had plenty, Glen, Hoyt, and John was shipping to Chicago. But they had plenty of greens. So General said "I will find out how many we are going to need from ya'll at least once a week." "I will let you know."

By now the businesses all had phones. Mr. General kind of made his phone headquarters at Mr. Sam's store. He went on back to the store and called Clarence back and said that they can handle the green deal. Clarence said he had a buddy in Cincinnati that was needing greens. General said he thought there was plenty to handle it. Clarence said he would need a load a week and the guy in Cincinnati would need a load a week. Of course General knew that Shorty's man in St Louis would need a load a week. Shorty made it on back in the next day. General got with him and told him what the deal was. Shorty said "Well Marty wants a full load every week." General said "Well I got that 10 wheeler." "We can load that for Cincinnati." "I don't know what we can do about the Louisville load." Shorty said "I know an old boy down there at Sayre that hauls coal." "I will go down there and check with him." "His name is Robbie Dale Wood." "I'll go down there and see." "If he has some high side boards he might want to haul them greens." General said that would be fine. "He can haul to Louisville to Clarence." "Harold can take my 10-wheeler and do Cincinnati and you can keep doing St Louis."

It was getting late but Shorty cut out down to Sayre to see if he could locate Robbie. At this time Robbie was about all he ever done was haul coal. It still was not far enough in the year to get real busy for hauling coal. Shorty and Robbie knew each other. Shorty finally located him down there. Shorty asked if he was getting to haul any coal and he said well I'm getting to haul a little. Not very busy right now. So Shorty told him what the deal was and asked him if he'd be interested in hauling a load of greens a week to Louisville. He asked him also if he had any high side boards. Robbie said "yeah I haul hay sometimes and my side boards are real tall." Shorty said" well if you're real interested in doing it I'll show you how and help you." "We can put those side boards on and we'll get some tar paper to tack on the inside to keep the air out." Shorty asked him if he had a tarp. Robbie said "yeah I got a real big tarp." Robbie acted like he was interested but wanted to hear all the details. Shorty told him what the deal was. His brother General was shipping greens to St Louis and fixing to start hauling to Louisville and needed someone to haul these. Robbie said is General your brother? He said "yeah." "Well I know General I met him down there on the market." "I haul coal sack coal down there to the market for them peddlers that have got a little truck." Shorty said "you can make pretty good money doing this." "You ought not to have any trouble hauling 250 bushel." "General will pay you a dollar a bushel." Shorty said "I've made them trips before on gas, eating, and cigarettes you not going spend over 50 dollars." "That would give you 200 dollars left in your pocket." "Even you have a little tire trouble, you still going to have 190 dollars left." Robbie said "that sounds good to me." "Said I can't do that in a week hauling coal even when it's real busy." Shorty said "yeah this is Monday so we will want to load Wednesday evening." "It might be late Wednesday evening up there in Garden City. "He told Robbie where he would need to be about the middle of the afternoon. Shorty said "if you need me I can come back down here and help you get your truck ready." Robbie said "no it's too far for you to drive back down here." "I got an old man that lives down there next to me that's not doing anything right now." "He'll be glad to help me and make him a few dollars." "I understand what you mean about getting it sealed with tar paper and have my tarp ready." So they sealed the deal and Shorty told him again where to be in Garden City around 2:30 in the afternoon and Robbie said he'd be there.

On the door of Robbie's truck he had Robbie Dale Wood Coal Hauling Sayre, AL. and on Shorty's truck he had Shorty Thomas Produce Bangor, AL. On General's truck he had General Thomas and Sons Orchards Bangor, AL. Shorty got on back home and got up Tuesday morning and went over to General's house. He told him had everything lined up to load greens on Wednesday afternoon. For him to get on and get the greens, his, Coy and Brady's, and the greens out of Corner so they could have everything there to load all three loads and can leave out of there Wednesday night.

CHAPTER FORTY-THREE
Just See What Happens

Now Shorty was keeping Cracker informed on what was going on. He told Cracker that they still wanted to use his crew to ice and load the trucks. This will give them a little work to do and would keep the farmer's from having to bring their crew in out of the fields. Cracker said Shorty that'll be fine. We will just rock along see what happens. It'll keep everything looking the same in town.

Now Cracker from what he had read and heard on the news from J Edgar Hoover that he still had people out there. He didn't know who or exactly who they were. He just knew that Hoover wasn't through looking. For a couple of days he had seen a couple of cub airplanes flying around in places where you hardly ever see one flying. Cracker got with Big George and told him. Big George said "Mr. Cracker I been seeing those planes too." "Look funny don't it" Cracker said "well we can't take any chances." "You get a bunch of your boys together and go over to the still." "Most of everything is under the rock bluff anyhow, but look and make sure that anything they might see and get suspicious of is under the bluff where they can't spot it. George said he would get it done."

Now General had went over to Corner and got with Glen and made the deal for him to furnish all he could and whatever else he needed to get from John and Hoyt. The deal was for them to cut 350 bushel and that he would send Shorty over there to load. Shorty could go by the ice house and get ice and he would pay them 25cents more for putting the ice in them and stack them on the truck. So he made that deal with Glen. That was going to through him and Coy to come up with 500 bushel of greens to load Harold and Robbie. They decided they couldn't come up with that many so he got with Jake and Dan Washburn, they had a patch of greens down on the river so he got with them and made a deal with them to cut 150 bushel.

Cracker got by Mr. Sam's store late Tuesday evening. He had gotten all his money in from Memphis and St Louis so he got by to straighten up with Mr. Sam. He still owed him about 800 dollars. He paid him off and Mr. Sam thanked him. Cracker said "well I don't think we will be needing anything right away." But Mr. Sam said "well that ain't no problem if you need something let me know."

Oak Grove Mountain got all their people in the field cutting the greens. They were going to have a big day. About 2 pm that afternoon Shorty headed for the ice house in Warrior to pick up the ice for the greens in Corner. Harold headed down there in General's 10-wheeler to pick up ice for the two loads to be loaded in Garden City. About 4:30 pm all the farmers started coming in with their greens. Jake and Dan got there first with theirs and got them unloaded on the dock. Then Coy and Brady got there and unloaded on the dock. Harold rolled in with the ice truck and then in a little while General came in with his load of greens. Since there wasn't any whiskey involved Cracker had Big George and his crew gets over there before dark to start getting the greens iced down.

They got everything lined up and got to icing and dipping the greens and started stacking them on the dock. About 5:00

pm Robbie come rolling in with his rig and had it ready to go. They went ahead and loaded Robbie truck first since Harold's truck had ice on it. Now Robbie and Harold hadn't never met they were both about 17 and 17 ½. Both full of Piss and Vinegar. They finally got both trucks loaded. Harold told Robbie not to put his top on that they had to go down to Warrior and put top ice on them. He said we will tarp down there. So they headed on down 31 hwy to Warrior. When they got down there Shorty had already got his top ice and was pulled over to one side tarping it down. Harold and Robbie got their load top ice and got the trucks tarpped down. Harold told Robbie "if you want me to I will lead the way." "I have been driving some through there since I was 15 years old." "Before then I made trips with my uncle Short and my daddy." Robbie said "yeah that will be fine." "I been to Nashville but I've never been to Louisville." So they rigged it up to where Harold was the lead driver.

About 12 or 12:30 they got up to right above the Tennessee line at Fayetteville, Tn. There was an all night Café there where they eat and gas up. They pulled in and got gassed up and pulled around to go in and eat to get them a hamburger. Hadn't either one of them had supper. They got them a burger and shot the bull a little bit and played the juke box while they were in there. They finally got through eating and got ready to go. They left this pretty good looking old girl, she was about 21 or 22 but to them she was old. They both left her a quarter. She thanked them and they said well we will see you in a few days. When they got out Harold told Robbie "if we will get on the ball we can get through Nashville before everybody gets up and out." "That will save us a lot of time." So they made it and they got on up there on the mountain above Nashville. Robbie was still trailing Harold. Then Harold blowed out a tire on the right tandem on the 10-wheeler. He didn't know it and Robbie was trying to get him to stop. Finally they got on a straight away and Robbie pulled in the left lane and kept flashing his lights. He finally got

Harold's attention so he pulled over. He had a spare so Robbie helped him get it jacked up. They took the tire off and put the spare on. Harold said "the market is about three blocks off of my route going to Cincinnati.' "Since you hadn't ever been there I'll go by there and show you where it's at." "There is an ice house there "said "I might need to put on a little more top ice."

Around 12:30 they made it in to Louisville. Harold went on around by the market to show Robbie where it was. So he also pulled his tarp back and decided he might need to put on about 600 hundred more pounds of top ice. He got ready to head on to Cincinnati. He hollered and told Robbie "when you get back in go by the house and Daddy will pay you." Robbie said "yeah I will but General has already given me a hundred dollars." "He wanted to make sure I had plenty of money." So Harold headed on out to Cincinnati.

Everything had gone so well with this run they decided to keep doing it for the next week. The farmers were selling their produce and this would only make the whiskey operation look more like a real honest operation.

CHAPTER FORTY-FOUR
Shorty Goes to Court

Now Shorty had decided that since he wasn't hauling no whiskey that he would run his old route across the river at Memphis on to Arkansas through Missouri and to St Louis. He liked running that route better then he did through Tennessee to Kentucky on to southern Illinois. He got onto the scales that night the Mississippi scales. His old buddies were there. They weighed him and they asked him what he had on. He said greens. One of them said well I sure could use some good turnip greens. Shorty well hop up there and get yall a bushel of them. Said they will be enough to give your neighbor some. He didn't wait on them to ask so he said Boys there want be no more shine. That old one pot moonshiner down there the law has been after him. They didn't get nobody but they busted his still up so it might be next spring before he can have anymore. They said they understood.

Shorty pulled out and headed on up the line. Shorty crossed the river up there at Memphis and run up the Arkansas side and Missouri. He got up to Cape Gerardo about 1:30 pm in the afternoon. He was easing through town and that cop spotted him. He let him get out of town before he pulled him over. He put the red light on him. Shorty pulled over and the cop came up there and asked him for his license. Shorty gave them to him. The cop said "yeah I thought this was the same truck." Shorty said "well what's wrong." That cop said "well nothing but I will find something." "You almost caused me to get fired." Shorty said "well what happened." He said "well I called all them agents up in Kansas City to be looking for you and you didn't ever show up and they came down here and wanted to charge me with lying to them and everything else." "How come you lie to me?" Shorty said "well I really didn't lie to you." "I got up there right out of St Louis and my truck started running hot on me and I called A&P and told them what the trouble was and where I was at." "I told them if they didn't care I would just try to move that load on the market at St Louis." "They said that wasn't no bad idea that if I missed the appointment up there that I might loose the whole load." The cop didn't much like what Shorty told him so he went to looking around trying to find something wrong. Finally he found a lug nut loose on the trailer axle back there. He said "Well Mr. Thomas I'm going to have to write you up for that." Shorty said "Well I'll be glad to send it in when I get back." The cop said "no you going to have to go in front of the judge and see what he says." Shorty said "well if that's what I got to do that's what we'll do." The cop wrote the ticket and loaded Shorty up in his car. They went down about 5 blocks to City Hall. The cop went in and told Shorty to sit down there right inside the door. He wanted to go in and see what was going on. In a little bit he came back out and said the judge is ready for you. You just walk right up there in front the judge knows all the details. So Shorty went in and he was in front of Judge Limbaugh. Old Judge Limbaugh was in there and he asked Shorty his name. Shorty told him. The Judge said "well Mr. Thomas how do you plea on this?" and Shorty replied "Well Judge I guess I'm guilty." "The lug nut was loose." Old Judge Limbaugh hit his gavel on the desk and said "that'll be 10 dollars but I ain't going to charge you no court cost." Shorty said "I sure do thank you sir." As Shorty was walking out of the City Hall he met a young woman carrying a baby. Shorty spoke to her and held the door open for her. She walked in with the baby. Judge Limbaugh said "Hey I heard we got us a boy. Did you name him after me?" She replied "No we are calling him Rush. The Judge said, "Hmm, Rush?" scratching his chin, "That Rush Limbaugh has a ring to it."

The cop got Shorty on back to the truck and let him take off. Shorty made it on in early to St Louis. The greens were red hot. They were selling like hot cakes in Louisville and Cincinnati also. This was because South Georgia had been real dry and was late coming in. The truck drivers made it on in back home. They started making plans for the next Wednesday. This thing went on about two more weeks just like clock work. Shorty, Robbie and Harold was a really hauling them greens.

All the farmers and the truckers made plans to get their greens out and make another load this coming Wednesday. All the plans were in the works. The Bagwell's over at Corner was getting their greens ready. Coy, Brady and General were going to have their greens ready so they could load three loads on Wednesday afternoon. Now Shorty on this last trip had promised to try and get them old scales boys a little more whiskey if they could. He told them he would do the best he could. So he made a trip over to the 78 strip and went in and talked to Bill Hollis. Hollis told him "Yea Shorty I can get you some if you hang around here awhile but it is tighter then it was. The moonshine market is tighter then it's been being." Of course Hollis and Shorty both knew why. So Shorty wound up getting them a couple more gallons of moonshine to carry to them on Wednesday night.

Well Wednesday finally rolled around and everybody got their greens out. Shorty went up to Warrior to pick up his ice to go over to Corner to get those greens. Harold went to get ice to pack the two loads going to Louisville and Cincinnati. Everything went real smooth and everybody got out real early.

Cracker had Big George to come in early so they could get the greens packed as early as possible. They got the work done and finished up Robbie and Harold's loads. Shorty got his load done over at Corner and headed to Warrior for more ice then north over to Jasper toward Memphis. Harold and Robbie got their loads iced and tarped down and headed toward Tennessee. That night around 1:00 or 2:00 in the morning Shorty got to the scales. His old buddies were there. They weighed and everything was good. He pulled off the scales and he told them he had the moonshine. They talked about this and that for a while and then Shorty told them by and headed on off to St Louis. Harold and Robbie got on up to the edge of Tennessee and the scales were open. It was about 12:30 am and they had to pull into weigh. The weight was alright but Harold had three or four clearance lights were out. That particular night the big man was there. The Interstate Commerce Commission better known as the ICC. The big man at the ICC told the head man at the scales that he was going to have to fine him and write him a ticket. "We got to get all this kind of stuff stopped."

So they were seeing to all of that and they knew what the trucks had on them. So eventually the ICC man left and all that was left were the two scale men. The head scale man asked Harold, "who is this shipping all these greens out of Bangor Alabama?" Harold said, "My daddy General Thomas." The head man replied, "General Thomas? Is he any kin to Shorty Thomas?" Harold said, "Yea that's my uncle." So the scale man went into the back room with his buddy and talked a few minutes and he said, "Man I ain't gonna give Shorty's nephew a ticket. Man as much watermelon, cantaloupe, peaches, and whiskey that Shorty has brought to us, No sir I ain't about to him no ticket." Harold never did know why he didn't give him a ticket. The scale man just came out and said as soon as the man got his lights fixed they were free to go. So they left and eased on up the road to the all night café and truck stop. They got fueled up and checked their water and tires and everything else. They pulled over to the side and went into the café and the old gal friend who was 22 years old she was in there waiting on them. They had a couple of burgers and played the juke box a little. Shot the bull awhile and then left to head on up toward Nashville and made it through before getting up time which saved them time. They made good time on up into Kentucky into Louisville. It was about 9:00 am when they got there and Harold decided he was going to go on and check his ice and make sure if he needed any top ice. He saw he needed some so while he was getting that Robbie came over and said "Harold they ain't no way I can drive back home after I get unloaded. I had to haul coal all day yesterday and worked all day before we left and I've drove all night and part of today so they ain't no way I can do it." Harold replied," Well they ain't no hurry for you to get back I'll go in here and get Clarence to unload the truck. You can ride with me and sleep and go on up to Cincinnati. You sleep while I drive and then on the way back I'll sleep while you drive." So Robbie liked that idea so they got Clarence lined up to unload and he told hi where he would leave the key. So they headed on up old turkey run to Cincinnati. Everything went real good. They got up there and the produce man in Cincinnati had held some help over to unload them so they got unloaded pretty fast. Robbie had slept for a while so he took over driving for Harold. They headed on back down turkey trot. Harold was getting him a little nap. They got on back down to Louisville and picked up Robbie's truck. Harold told him "Now, Robbie there is a truck stop down about 50 miles south on the mountain. We are both still tired so let's get on down there and eat and then we will lay down in their bunk house and sleep awhile." Robbie really liked that idea so they got on down there.

They got in there and gassed up and went in to eat. As they sat around there they talked about how long they had been up and going without sleep. There was an old truck driver in there about

45; they thought he was old compared to them. He told them, "Now boys you got to sleep some but I am going to tell you how to get on down to Alabama without having a wreck. Go on and sleep three or four hours and then get up and come in and buy you a pack of Picayune Cigarettes and smoke several of these." "They're very strong and will keep you awake." So they went on into the bunkhouse and slept awhile. When they got up they went and bought a pack of the cigarettes. They drank coffee and smoked for about an hour. So they decided to get up to leave and head toward the truck. The man who owned the café saw them heading out the door toward their trucks. They barely could walk. They were staggering like they was drunk. So he went out there and asked them where they was heading. They said with a smile, "We headed to Birmingham hammer down." He said "no you're not leaving my truck stop like that." "Ya'll act like ya'll been dranking whiskey. Ya'll look like your drunk." They said "No sir," and they told him what the old driver had said about smoking them picayune cigarettes. He said, "Well you're going to sleep awhile longer before you leave."

So they slept awhile longer and it was up after daylight before they headed home. By that time Mr. General was worried about them. He went over to Mr. Sam's store and called Cincinnati and they told him they had unloaded and were together when they left there. So he called Clarence Mayfield in Louisville. He told him they had left the truck and went on together. He told him that they had come back by and picked up the truck so they were somewhere down the road. Well they finally rolled in about 8:00 pm that night. Mr. General went out to check on them and asked them "Where have you boys been. What happen?" Robbie said, "Well, Mr. General we got drunk." Mr. General said, "What did you do? I'm going to tear ya'll up. Don't think you're too big to get your asses beat." Harold started laughing and then explained what had happened. Then Mr. General made them get in the house eat some supper and go to bed.

Now Shorty on his trip up had taken care of everything at the scale and made it on up to Cape Gerardo. Shorty saw his old scale buddy, the one who had stopped him earlier, sitting on the side of the road so he waived at him and blowed his air horn. So Shorty got to thinking and grinning to himself well maybe well I've just made a good buddy out of him.

CHAPTER FORTY-FIVE

The Accident

This was getting on into November. Early Thursday morning Mr. Sam was going into Hayden to Henry and Homer Standridge's to carry them some sugar. He was the sugar supplier. Little Ben was going with him so they headed to Hayden that morning. They got down there and made their delivery so they were heading on back to Garden City. They would have to cross the railroad tracks up there at Bangor. They were coming on down through there it was rainy and cold that day so they had the windows up tight. Mr. Sam had his mind on something else and was not really paying attention to what he was doing. He came onto the railroad track and there was a southbound freight train coming real fast. He didn't hear the train. It hit them and drug them down the track about ¾ mile before the truck came loose from the train. When the people got there to find out what happened Little Ben was dead. They got Mr. Sam out he was hurt real bad. They took him to the hospital in Cullman. When the news got out about the wreck everybody was really hurt and sad because everybody new Mr. Sam and Little Ben. Now Ms. Clara was a real strong woman so she got with Ben and Little Ben's momma. She talked to them a little while before she went on to the hospital. She wanted them to know she would take care of everything.

Some people there in town took Ms. Clara to the hospital to see Mr. Sam. When she got there Mr. Sam was conscious and thought he knew everything but, didn't know for sure that Little Ben was dead. He asked Ms. Clara about Little Ben and she told him that Little Ben was dead. That really hurt him and messed him up. In a little bit he asked for Ms. Clara to come back in he wanted to talk to her. So they called her back in. He wanted her to ask Big Ben and Little Ben's mother if they could bury Little Ben in their plot at the cemetery. Ms. Clara said she would ask them.

So late that afternoon, Ms. Clara went on back to Garden City to take care of things that needed to be done. She was going to see about Big Ben and Little Ben's momma. She asked them to come to the store she wanted to talk to them. So they came over to the store and she told them what Mr. Sam wanted to do and was that alright she also told them that there would also be room in their plot for them to be buried. So Ruthie and Big Ben told her yes that if that's what Mr. Sam wants to do we will do it. At about midnight that night Mr. Sam Died. The hospital had called Ms. Clara but, by the time she got there he had passed away.

The word got around for the plans for the funeral and everything. The whole community was glad that Little Ben would be buried in the cemetery. But the word got down to Bangor to the Reno's that Little Ben would be buried in the white cemetery with Mr. Sam and they didn't like that. So they got with their buddies the McKenzie's and on Friday night they stopped in at Ms. Clara's house and knocked on the door. She had Ruthie and Ben with her they were staying together. She went to the door and the head Reno told her "Ms. Clara there ain't going to be no nigger boy buried in the white graveyard." She told him that was Mr. Sam's last request and that's what we going to do. So the Reno's left.

It bothered Ruthie, Big Ben and Ms. Clara but, they were still going to do it. So the next morning early Ms. Clara sent word for

Cracker to come and talk to her. Cracker was a real good friend. They had a lot of friends in town but, Cracker was a special friend she knew she could depend on. So Cracker got over there about 8:30 that morning. Ms. Clara told him that the Reno's had come up there and said there would not be any nigger boys buried in the white cemetery. Cracker told her "you don't worry about nothing." "You go on with you plans and don't worry." "If you need help with anything else let me know." "You, Mr. Sam, Big Ben and Ruthie are some of the best friends I've ever had." "You just don't worry about nothing."

Cracker went on and talked to George Harden a little while. He then went on and got with Big George and told him kindly what the story was and that he wanted him Little Willie and at least 5 or 6 of his workers to come to the funeral. He wanted them to be close by to him in case they were needed.

Big Ben, Ruthie and Ms. Clara got with the undertakers and made all the funeral plans. The funeral would be at the church Sunday at 2:00 pm. Ms. Clara got the word out that she wanted to make sure that all the black people was welcome to come to the church. Sunday morning finally rolled around and it was real cold, rainy and foggy that day. About 11:00 people started coming in to attend the funeral. The hearse arrived and they began to carry the caskets in for the funeral. There was a good many blacks there but, there was more whites. They got everybody in and had a song or two and then the pastor of the church got up and spoke. In a little bit the black pastor got up and spoke. He put his hands together and said in this world this is the way Mr. Sam and Little Ben were. They will also be this way in heaven. They had some more songs and completed the funeral. They came on out to the grave site. There were a lot of people there that day.

They all gathered around the grave site and got lined up to have the graveside service. They were getting started when three old cars rolled up. It was the Reno's and McKenzie's. They all got out carrying big sticks. They walked up pretty close and the head Reno stepped out in front and said "Now Ms. Clara I told you there wasn't going to be no nigger boy buried in the white cemetery." Ms. Clara told him said "Well son this was Mr. Sam's last request." "I am running things around here now and that is what we are going to do." The Reno's started easing on in a little closer. They looked up and looked surprised. There eyes got real big and they took off running as fast as they could toward their cars. What they were seeing was twelve Ku Klux in full dress easing out of the fog up behind the funeral party. They came up close enough to where you could barely see them. Most of the funeral attendees couldn't see them and didn't know what was going on because they never had turned around and looked. So they went on with the service and the preachers had their say. They sang a song or two and then they sang "Farther Along." Into the song Big Liza, a big heavy set black woman from the cotton patch stepped out in front and took over the song. She began singing in her rich contralto voice. Her singing could be heard for miles around. As she sang from her heart she began to get the Holy Ghost and was really singing and dancing and pouring it on. Everyone there began to be moved by the Holy Ghost and sang along with Big Liza. This is the way it should have been, Mr. Sam and Little Ben sitting side by side on the bank of the river that never runs dry.